I0547781

The Refusal

by Julie L. Spencer

Copyright © 2021 Spencer Publishing, LLC

All rights reserved. No part of this book may be reproduced in any form or by any means without written permission.

All characters in this book are fictitious, and any resemblance to actual persons, living or dead, is purely coincidental.

www.AuthorJulieSpencer.com

ISBN: 978-1-954666-11-5

CONTENTS

Note to Readers

Falling in love is the greatest feeling in the world. That's why I write romance and love stories. The day I met my husband I looked across the room at him and knew I was going to marry him. I didn't know his name (it's Clayton), I didn't know how old he was (nine months older than me), or if he was dating anyone (he was). All I knew was I was going to marry him. Almost twenty-five years later we're still on our honeymoon. Because that is my experience with falling in love, my characters tend to fall in love just as quickly. Love grows over time, but sometimes you look at someone and just *know* they are your person. You can call it Instalove, Love-at-First Sight, whatever you want. I pray that everyone in the world experiences the kind of love I feel every time I look into the eyes of my eternal companion.

God bless you, my friends. Stay safe! -Julie

Dedication

Dedicated to Troy…
even though he'll probably never read this.

Chapter One—First Refusal

"It's a good job, Mom." Melissa pushed another pile of clothes into her suitcase and strode across her room. She had barely unpacked the jeans and sweatshirts from college before loading up slacks and professional blouses. She hesitated as she held up her favorite Brigham Young University sweatshirt, then shoved it back into the suitcase, along with her nicest pair of jeans. "Don't you want me to have a good job?"

"I just want you to be happy. Is this really the life you envisioned for yourself?" Jan Dalton, Melissa's mom, sat on the edge of the twin bed. She glanced around Melissa's childhood bedroom and fidgeted with a loose thread on the comforter. "Working at a hardware store?"

"Farm and Tractor Supply is hardly *just* a hardware store! We provide premium quality supplies to the rural community in a way that no other store can compete with. I've worked for the company all through college, and we're farmers for heaven's sake. You and Daddy have practically raised me to have this job."

"You sound like a walking commercial."

"I'm passionate about what we do." Melissa held up two pairs of shoes—one that went with every dressy outfit she owned, from church clothes to work slacks, and the other a casual pair of loafers. She tucked them both into her suitcase and threw in her work boots for good measure. Then she realized she should have a grubby pair of jeans and a flannel shirt as well. That led to a few of her favorite T-shirts. Before she knew it, she had repacked half the clothes she'd brought home from college.

"But being a store manager is a huge responsibility," her mom said.

"I've been an assistant store manager for almost two years, and pretty much ran the place while Donna was on maternity leave. I know what I'm doing, and I'm excited to transfer over here."

"But rural Michigan is not the same as Utah." Her mom shook her head and sighed.

"I grew up in rural Michigan. Right here in this house. On a farm. With farmers, remember?"

"Northern Michigan is not the same. You're heading south. They're different down there."

"It's beautiful down there. Rolling hills to the west. Open farmland to the east. Cornfields and sugar beets as far as the eye can see. My new office overlooks a pasture with horses so beautiful it takes your breath away. At my interview, I felt like I had finally found my home."

"But it's so desolate," her mom whispered, apparently forgetting that Lowell was a suburb of Grand Rapids, the second largest city in Michigan. "How are you ever going to find a husband all the way down there?"

"That's what this is really about, isn't it?" Melissa stopped packing and sat on the bed next to her mom. "You're still upset that I'm not marrying Andy."

"He was a good man. Your refusal devastated him. He would have made a fine husband."

"He didn't love me." Melissa felt the heat rush to her cheeks. "And I didn't love him."

"You did at one time…"

"He only wanted me as a trophy wife, to show me off. He called me 'Eye Candy' to his friend. I heard him say it. I don't want to be sought after just because I'm beautiful. I want to be loved for who I am on the inside."

"You can't get around that, Melissa." Her mom's brow furrowed. "You've always been a beauty, and you'll always *be* my gorgeous little girl. Your looks will always be the first thing men notice. It's inevitable. But I understand your frustration. I'm sure, when the time comes, you'll meet someone who will see inside and fall in love with your fiery, confident personality… he may need to be blind…"

"Well, gee, maybe there's a blind guy down there just waiting for a fiery, passionate, confident farm girl." Melissa nudged her mom with her shoulder. "You know, I've prayed about this decision. I know this is where God wants me to be at this time in my life, and I'm going to keep my beautiful green eyes open to the possibilities. But I'm honestly not looking for a husband right now. I'm just going to have fun living with my cousin, going to church with her every Sunday, letting her drag me around to meet every young single adult in the Grand Rapids area, enjoying my new job, and finding my place in this world. Finding a husband will have to wait."

Melissa stood and finished packing, ignoring her mom until she finally left the room.

* * * * * * * *

"Blasted!" Troy kicked the tire on his no-till planter, where his drive chain had jammed right at the edge of the field. He crouched and picked up the piece of broken glass that was the culprit. The late-morning sun warmed his back, reminding him that his perfect day was just ruined by some irresponsible kids throwing beer bottles in his fields again. Troy mumbled under his breath, "Seeds won't get in the ground without a working drill."

Troy waved to his brother in the next field over, holding up his roller chain. Craig climbed down from the tractor and came over to investigate the broken links. "Guess we're gonna need to make a trip into town."

"I don't have *time* for this!" Troy hauled back his arm as if he was going to chuck the piece of glass as far as he could throw it, then stopped himself at the last second, realizing that wherever it landed would cause more problems at a later date. Instead, he tucked it into the pocket of his jeans, brushed off his hands, and started toward the truck. His eyes lifted to the clear, blue sky, and he started grumbling. "Rain's going to be here in a day or two, and I won't have my beans in the ground. This is just perfect. Can't get a break."

"You need to relax." Craig rushed to catch up with him and laid his hand on Troy's shoulder, slowing him down. "We'll get done in time."

"You're just glad we got your fields done yesterday." Troy pushed his brother's hand away and climbed into the driver's side of his new Ford F-450. The keys were already in the ignition. This far out of town, anyone close enough to steal his truck was probably related to him and wouldn't dare. He cranked the ignition and let the purr of the engine lull him out of his bad mood. The new car smell rushed from the air conditioner, reminding him what a good choice he'd made at the dealership. He ran his hand along the dashboard.

As Craig climbed up into the passenger side of the cab, he raised his eyebrows and smirked suggestively. "You know, if you would just marry Becca, you wouldn't need to have an improper relationship with your new truck."

"I don't wanna marry Becca." Troy ground his teeth together and pouted.

"You know she's the girl Father chose for you…"

"I don't care." Troy put the truck in reverse and backed out of the drive. "Don't I get a choice in the matter?"

"That's not the way it works in the Mennonite church," Craig reminded him. "It's time you grow up

11

and accept your responsibilities as a Brother in the faith."

"I'm not ready to grow up yet." A devious grin threatened the corners of Troy's mouth. He shifted the truck into gear and peeled out of the drive, fishtailing the back end and spraying gravel over the edge of the field.

"Geesh! Let me at least get my seat belt on!"

Troy knew his brother wasn't really mad at him for driving like a daredevil. The smile plastered on Craig's face as he held the grab bar above the door told Troy everything he needed to know. He cranked the steering wheel back and forth one more time, leaving ruts in the field.

"Dad's going to kill you!" Craig hollered above the country music blaring from the stereo.

"It's *my* field now. I can do what I want with it." Troy hollered back.

"Dad's been cultivating those fields longer than we've been alive, and when are you going to grow up and quit listening to that horrible music?"

"I'll grow up when I'm good and ready." Troy smirked at his older brother. "You were just as much a rebel when you were my age." Craig smiled back, and they raised their arms, bumping fists in solidarity.

"Good thing you don't have a family to feed. You'd be taking better care of your soil."

"That reminds me." Troy turned off the radio, knowing his brother would appreciate it. His speed slowed to a more reasonable fifteen miles per hour over the speed limit, and he creased his eyebrows. "Is little Jesse feeling better? Did he get over his cough? I'm sorry I forgot to ask this morning."

"You've been a little distracted," Craig acknowledged. "Yes, he's fine. Nothing that can't be fixed with a little homemade chicken soup and Jessica's loving arms."

"Must be nice to be married." Troy sighed. He did want that. He just didn't want it with Becca. He couldn't understand why no one else in the community couldn't see that. She was more like a sister to him. He wasn't even remotely attracted to her in a physical way. Yet she followed him around at church, dropping hints about how nice his house was coming along and how she couldn't wait to see what it looked like on the inside. It was as if she, and everyone else, was just assuming that one day he would turn around, look down into her big brown eyes, and realize that she was the perfect girl to come and sew some curtains to hang in his new kitchen.

"Watch it, little brother!" Troy snapped out of his daydream soon enough to swerve off the shoulder of the road. "You won't live long enough to get married if you don't learn how to drive."

"I'll show you how to drive." Troy grinned and sped up again, making it to Farm and Tractor Supply in record time.

Chapter Two—Farm Boy

"Dang, why's this place so busy on a Wednesday morning with the sun shining?" Troy wrinkled his brow and pursed his lips, looking at the café, where a few old men usually hung out to drink burnt coffee and talk about the weather.

It wasn't really a café in the literal sense, it was just a sitting area with a couple of tables next to a counter filled with complimentary donuts and bagels. Sometimes he wondered if the guys didn't come here more for the camaraderie and free pastries than to get supplies.

That day, there were at least twice the number of men sitting around, and many of them were much younger than the usual crowd. He shook his head and started toward the counter so he could inquire about getting a new drive chain. A strange conversation caught his attention, and he halted in his tracks, listening to a familiar male voice in the next aisle.

"Since yer new in town, yer gonna need someone to show you around. I could take you for a drive in my new Chevy and give you the grand tour."

"Thank you," a woman replied. "I'm sure I can find my way around just fine." The curt tone of the voice spoke volumes. She wasn't interested in his advances.

Troy decided to play the gentleman and rescue the damsel, whoever she was. He came around the corner

14

and stepped behind a woman with long strawberry blonde hair, barely glanced at her but made firm eye contact with his archenemy.

"You know, Dean, I don't think the lady is interested in riding around in a *Chevy* truck." Troy leaned against the shelving unit, putting a tiny bit of space between the woman and her pursuer.

"What's it to *you*, farm boy?" Dean took a step toward Troy, who straightened his stance protectively. "You think she's gonna wanna ride around in yer fancy new Ford?"

"Thank you for the compliment, Dean," Troy said. "But I think the lady can find her way home in whatever car she drove here this morning."

Craig came up behind his brother, and Dean took a step back, narrowing his eyes.

They stood there a moment more, three men staring one another down, and one woman with her arms crossed and her chin raised. Dean was the first to back down.

"Whatever, farm boy." Dean tossed the bag of lug nuts on the shelf and walked away.

"Thank you," the woman said with annoyance, finally turning to Troy and Craig. The hardness in her eyes startled Troy. He expected her to be grateful for his defense. Instead, she looked offended. "I'm pretty sure I can take care of myself from now on."

"Uh... I'm sorry"—Troy read her temporary name tag and realized she was probably a new employee at the store—"Melissa. I was just trying to help. I didn't mean to make you more upset."

Melissa shook her head, rolled her eyes, and turned around, confidently walking away. He hurried to keep up with her.

"Look, the guy's a jerk, okay? He needed to be put in his place. He can't just think he can make advances at any ol' woman he wants."

Troy halted when she suddenly turned to face him, eyes narrowed, stance firm, arms crossed.

Crud, I've offended her again. "Not that you're old. That's not what I meant. You're… I don't know how old you are… but you're definitely not old. It's just that… it's not about you. It's about Dean. He's a jerk."

"You said that already." She lifted her eyebrows. "The feelings must be mutual because he sure doesn't seem to like you either… farm boy."

"Eh… I stole his prom date once, and he's never forgiven me." That brought a little smile. "I'm kidding. We didn't even go to the same high school. Plus, I've never actually dated a girl before. He just doesn't like me because I called the cops on him for setting a field on fire when he was drunk one night a few summers back."

By that time, Melissa was openly laughing at him, and Troy realized he was rambling. He stopped, took a deep breath, and shoved his hands into his pockets. His finger sliced against the glass, and he pulled out the broken piece of beer bottle.

The Refusal

Troy held up the piece of glass with his right hand and stuck the side of his bleeding finger into his mouth. He cringed at the taste of blood mixed with manure and spit it back out, wiping his mouth on his sleeve and wrapping his finger in the hem of his shirt.

"I need a new drive chain for my drill." Troy tried not to gag, wishing he could run over and take a swig out of one of those cups of burnt coffee just to get the flavor of manure out of his mouth.

"It looks more like you need a bandage than a chain," Melissa said in a fake southern accent.

"Yes, please." Troy nodded. "That, and I need to wash the manure off my hands, and somehow get the taste out of my mouth."

"Come on." She grabbed his shirtsleeve and playfully dragged him over to the counter, where she opened the cooler of sodas and grabbed him a Coke. After shoving it into his hand, she led him farther back to a storage room.

Troy twisted the cap off the Coke and swigged half of it down as he walked straight over to a washbasin. He held his bleeding finger under cold running water.

Without hesitation, Melissa scrubbed Troy's filthy hands against a bar of soap.

Troy held very still. This was different from when his mom used to scrub his hands. Melissa probably didn't see it that way, but to him it felt almost suggestive. Too soon, she turned off the water and calmly wrapped his hands in a cloth towel. He watched her walk away, but she didn't go far.

From a cabinet nearby, she pulled out a small first-aid kit and rummaged around until she found a bandage. Almost mechanically, she pulled the towel aside and unwrapped the bandage, carefully pulling the little plastic tabs and sealing away the blood.

Troy almost felt as if he were going to fall over, not from the loss of what little blood had flowed from his finger, but from the way it felt to have her caring for him. He wanted to sigh with contentment but, instead, cleared his throat and took a step back.

"There, you're all better." She smiled up at him, clearly not as affected by the situation as he was. "Now, let's go find you that… chain."

Her eyes finally met his, and she didn't look away. In the low light of the utility room, her eyes shone like emeralds. The fluorescent lights cast shadows across her strawberry blonde hair, turning it a classic shade of mahogany. Troy had the uncanny desire to grasp one of the long curls between his fingers to see if it felt as soft as it looked. Thankfully, the throbbing in his hand, and his strict upbringing reminded him to show a little more restraint. He shook his head and looked away, breaking the spell.

"Yes," he whispered. "A chain. I came in here for a drive chain." His breathing was heavy and fast, and he could tell hers was as well.

She took one last deep breath, said, "Let's go find you that drive chain," then walked from the storeroom.

He watched her walk away, whispered, "As you wish," and quickly followed.

"What are you doing, Troy?" Craig asked, still standing near the door of the storeroom, arms crossed and furrowed brow.

"Buyin' a chain…" Troy barely acknowledged his brother as he walked past and followed Melissa.

Chapter Three—Playing with Fire and Soil

"Wish I'd cut *my* finger." A guy named Steve walked over from the café and leaned his arm against Troy's shoulder. Troy was still in a near trance when he wandered over to the other guys, carrying his newly purchased drive chain. Steve was a year younger than Troy but had played basketball at the local high school and had quite a height advantage. Troy barely noticed the weight on his shoulder. All the guys watched him, with jealousy in their eyes, but Steve was the only one who spoke up. "I see you've met our new store manager."

"Store manager?" Troy spun around and found Melissa's eyes again from across the room. One corner of her mouth turned up slightly as if she was encouraging him to come back anytime he needed another chain... or any other supplies for that matter.

"Lucky son of a gun." Steve sighed.

With that, Craig grabbed Troy's arm and pulled him out the door, new drive chain and all.

"You're playing with fire, little brother." Craig grabbed the keys out of his hand and led Troy over to the passenger side of his own truck. Troy didn't even hesitate. He wasn't sure he could find his way home. He was afraid if he had control of the wheel, he might turn his truck around. "She won't fit into your world. She's a rich college grad, and you're a poor farm boy."

"Excuse me," Troy corrected him. "I think the fully-loaded fifty-thousand-dollar truck you're driving and the hundred and sixty acres of land we're about to plant speaks differently. I am *not* a poor farm boy, and I don't care how much education or money she has or doesn't have, she's just plain Melissa to me."

"But she's *not* plain, Troy." Craig took his eyes off the road long enough to look over at his brother. His eyes held a firmness that bordered on disciplinary. Troy pulled his gaze away and stared out the window, allowing the rows of freshly planted fields to distract him from his brother's accusing glare. "Didn't you get a good look at her? She's not plain at all."

"What if I don't care that she's not plain? Huh? Did you think of that? What if I don't care what she looks like?" Troy lowered his voice to a near whisper. "You probably didn't notice how good she smelled."

"No, I'm sure I didn't." Craig pulled Troy's left hand from where it was resting on his leg. "I didn't have her groping me like you did."

"Groping me? She was washing my hands!" Troy yanked his arm away.

"I think… just maybe… at twenty-three years old… you know how to wash your own hands." Craig turned forward again, driving carefully to the field to repair the no-till drill, and Troy turned defiantly to stare out the passenger-side window.

* * * * * * * * *

The store closed at nine o'clock and Melissa fumbled with the keys, listening as her employee, Kathy chatted on about the guy she was going to meet at the bar that night. As they walked away from the building, they both halted when they noticed a man leaning against a dark blue truck parked next to their cars. His arms were crossed, and a soft smile played across his face, accentuating his neatly trimmed beard. Melissa's stomach flipped.

"Why, Troy Weller." Kathy's tone was flirtatious. "What on earth are you doing back here again?" She put her hands on her hips and flipped her hair, then hesitated when it was clear Troy never even glanced at her. His eyes were firmly locked with Melissa's.

"Good evening, Kathy." Troy still had not taken his eyes off Melissa.

"Well, gosh…" Kathy stammered. "Look at the time. I'm going to be late for my date. I'll leave the two of you to… uh… get acquainted. See you tomorrow, boss."

"Please don't call me that." Melissa didn't look away from Troy, but her request was not hesitant. She intended to start things off right with her employees, and chumming around wasn't in her plans.

"Sorry," Kathy said. She dug through her purse for her car keys, then climbed in and drove away without another word. Melissa hesitantly stepped the last ten feet forward.

"What *are* you doing here… Troy?"

"What? No more *farm boy*?" His voice was husky and soft. "I had to see you again."

"Why?"

"Because I didn't get a good enough look at you earlier today."

Melissa crossed her arms and huffed, highly doubting he hadn't looked at her. He had stared into her eyes in a way that allowed her to see almost clear to his soul.

"My brother told me I was blinded by the way you made me feel." Troy looked down at the pavement and shuffled his foot. He glanced up at her, his light brown eyes darkened by the casting shadows of twilight. "But I told him I was blinded by the way you smelled."

"So now I'm old *and* I smell bad?" Melissa teased.

"Oh, my heavens, definitely not!" Troy chuckled. He let out a long breath and shook his head. "And here I stood there smelling like manure."

"You didn't smell like manure to me," Melissa whispered. "You smelled like soil. There's a difference. And maybe a little like sweat."

"It was rather hot earlier today."

"It kinda still is…"

"But I showered off all the sweat and soil… hey did you say I smelled like soil?"

"Yeah, why?"

"Most people would call it dirt."

"My daddy would've hog-tied me and thrown me in the swine barn if I'd called it dirt."

"A woman after my own heart." Troy spoke reverently. "I think I'd like to meet your dad someday."

Melissa gulped and took a step back.

"Hey, I didn't mean it that way." Troy held out his hands, halting the line of thought. "Sorry, we got off on the wrong foot."

"More like the wrong hand," Melissa said. She picked up his bandaged hand and held it up in the waning light. She noticed he had replaced the bandage she'd applied with a new one, probably after his evening shower. She couldn't help recognize that he no longer smelled like sweat or soil. More like a natural musky scent mixed with a tasteful dash of cologne. She took a deep breath before asking if his hand was feeling better.

"It's feeling much better." He turned his wrist so she wasn't holding his hand, rather he was holding hers.

Having Troy hold her hand evoked very different feelings than when Andy had. Andy's caresses had been superficial, almost forced. As if he didn't want to touch her any more than she wanted to touch him. This was new and different, and a little frightening.

From Troy, she felt a hunger. She saw it in his eyes as well. She sensed he felt that same hunger from her. She knew she needed to get away from him immediately, before she did something crazy like reach up on her toes toward those full, softly-parted lips and brush hers against them.

The Refusal

Melissa pulled away, suddenly realizing she had almost done just that. She had almost kissed him. She released his hand and stepped quickly away while fumbling with her keys. She rushed around the car and hopped in. After tearing out of the parking lot, she pushed the accelerator to the floor of her little sedan. *I almost kissed him.*

Chapter Four—You Smell Like a Rose

"Ms. Dalton?" A light tap on her open door drew her attention away from the computer screen, where she had been tracking inventory and preparing an invoice. One of her employees stood in the doorway, with a tiny smile playing on his lips. "You have a… delivery."

"Can't Benjamin handle it in receiving?" She cocked her head to the side.

"This one requires your signature, and it came to the front desk, not out back."

Melissa was intrigued but took a few seconds to close out the screens and lock her computer. At the counter stood a delivery man from the local flower shop, holding a single pink rose and a tiny note. She hesitated, took a deep breath, confidently squared her shoulders, and felt her face flush, knowing every man in the café was watching to see her reaction. She looked up at the delivery man.

"Do you really need my signature for this?"

"No, not really." He shook his head. "The gentleman just asked me to make sure I hand it directly to you and not just leave it on the counter."

"Thank you, Dave." She read the embroidered name on his polo shirt. She held the rose close to her face to allow for the obligatory sniff test, then opened the little card. No name. Just a phone number and a single,

26

carefully scrawled word.

Dinner?

Melissa allowed a tiny smile to creep across her face, knowing every guy in the building wanted to see her face when she read the note, then turned and walked back to her office without saying another word or glancing at them.

She sat in her rolling chair, leaned back, and glanced out the window. She closed her eyes and held the rose to her face again, drinking in the aroma. Then she pulled herself forward and reached for her cell phone. *One quick text and then it's back to work.*

She hit *send* and logged into her computer. *Still think I smell bad, huh?*

*   *   *   *   *   *   *   *

That one text led to a back & forth conversation that lasted all afternoon. Melissa found it easier to talk to Troy if she wasn't distracted by his light brown eyes and sandy-colored hair. He was planting, but modern technology allowed a farmer to sit in an air-conditioned cab and let the tractor do most of the work.

By the time nine o'clock rolled around, Melissa had shared half her life story, and she had a working knowledge of Troy's crop rotation, the layout of all 160 acres of his fields, the names of the twelve chickens that roamed freely in his yard, and the dimensions of every room in the new house he was building near the little village of Pratt Lake. She'd never been to Pratt Lake, but suddenly had a strong desire to drive out into the country and see the landscape.

By the time she got done working, it was too late for dinner, so they settled for an ice cream cone and a stroll through downtown Lowell. The old Historical Museum rose majestically from the town square, casting shadows on the little building next door. They walked past closed storefronts along the cobblestone street and came to the corner near the fire station.

"See that little restaurant?" Troy pointed down the street at the side of a brick building.

"Brickstone Oven? Is it a bakery?"

"Sort of," he answered, then began to pull her back the way they'd come. "They make a great chicken salad and have the best pot roast you've ever tasted. We should go to lunch next week."

"Are you asking me on a date, Mr. Weller?" She pretended to be coy and even batted her eyelashes at him.

"I believe I am, Ms. Dalton."

"Well, I accept. What day should we go?"

"It's supposed to rain on Monday…" Troy suggested.

"The place will be pretty packed then." She looked up at him and pursed her lips slightly.

"That's good. You'll have a chance to meet the whole community."

"I think half the town's been sitting in the little café most mornings." Melissa kicked a little rock, and it tumbled a few feet ahead of them, resting near the gutter. "I think I've already met half the community."

Troy tapped the little rock with his foot, and it fell over the side of the curb. He faked a country drawl and bumped her shoulder. "Well, then you'll get to meet the other half." He cleared his throat and apologized. "I'll be kind of busy over the weekend with family stuff, but I'll pick you up a little before noon on Monday, okay? Get a table before the crowds invade."

"Is it that good of a bakery that there will be crowds?"

"You never know…" He chuckled. "It *is* going to rain." He walked her back to where they'd parked their cars and held open her door like a gentleman. He shut her into her car, and she thought she saw him wink just slightly as he took a step back. She smiled, started the ignition, and pulled slowly from the parking lot with a content sigh and a soft grin on her face.

Chapter Five—Girl Power

"This guy sounds kind of dreamy," her cousin, Jaimie said, teasing Melissa as they drove to church on Sunday.

"Dreamy? Really? What decade are we living in?" Melissa chuckled and looked away but whispered under her breath. "But yeah. He kind of is…" She was enjoying living with her cousin but had barely seen her since she'd moved in on Monday.

Melissa had been at the store from the time it opened until the time it closed every day all week, trying to acclimate herself to the way her new building was normally run. So far, she hadn't seen any major changes she wanted to make to their work environment. The previous manager had done a good job of keeping things running smoothly, and Melissa believed in the philosophy of not trying to fix what wasn't broken.

"Are you nervous that he isn't a member of our church?" Jaimie asked. "Does he even go to a church? Maybe you should invite him to come with us next week."

"We haven't talked about religion at all." Melissa played with the hem of her blouse.

"You turned down a perfectly good returned missionary at BYU to come home to Michigan and marry a country boy from the middle of nowhere."

"One, I'm not *marrying* him! We met less than a week ago." Melissa snapped her head toward her cousin, heat rushing to her cheeks. "And two, Andy and I were not in love. I'm not going to marry a guy just because he's a good guy. You sound like my mother."

"Oh, that's right," Jaimie taunted. "Your mom told my mom that he was just marrying you for your body and good looks."

"I don't even think he wanted my body," Melissa admitted. "He just wanted me on his arm at social events."

"I think I *want* to find a guy who wants me for my body. Twenty-five years is a little long to wait for… you know… some action."

"Jaimie!" Melissa smacked her cousin's leg. "You're scandalous!"

"What? You're saying you're not looking forward to rolling around in the hay a little with your cute farm boy?"

"Stop!" Melissa turned away and bit her lip, trying not to smile. She tried to compose herself. "I have dated farm boys most of my life, and I have never once wanted to…"

"Never once?" Jaimie smirked.

"Okay, okay, I felt a little heat from Troy last week when he was holding my hand in the parking lot at the store." She spoke really fast and tried to pretend she didn't know her face was turning beet red. "But that was the first time! Ever."

31

"Ever?"

"Yes, ever!" Melissa tried to stop smiling, but it wasn't working. "We are on our way to church for heaven's sake. You need to stop talking about this."

"Don't worry," Jaimie said, turning her car into the church parking lot. She blinked her eyelashes innocently. "You can just repent of your impure thoughts while you're taking the sacrament in a few minutes."

"You are *so* bad." Melissa laughed and reached into the back seat for her purse and scripture bag. The whole conversation gave Melissa a reason to reflect on the way she and Troy had gotten to know each other. They'd connected on a deeper level because they'd taken a step back to really talk. Texting all afternoon, holding hands and walking together, talking about everything and nothing. She was falling for him. Hard.

"Seriously though," Jaimie pointed out. She put her hand gently on Melissa's arm. "Don't you think it's a little telling that Troy is the first guy to make you feel this way?"

Melissa bit her lip and smiled softly. "Yeah, maybe it is."

* * * * * * * *

"Want to go for a drive in the country after church?" Melissa wagged her eyebrows and grinned conspiratorially at her cousin.

"Let me guess, you want to drive down to Pratt Lake? Do you even know where he lives?" Jaimie climbed into her car and strapped herself into her seat belt.

"No, not exactly… Well, not at all. I just want to get the lay of the land, so to speak."

"Nothing but a bunch of Mennonite farms down that way," Jaimie said. "But hey, he's a farmer. He ought to fit right in, right?"

"Right," Melissa said. "This is gonna be fun."

They drove south out of Lowell, then turned east, and wandered aimlessly, munching on granola bars and tortilla chips; windows down, breezes in their hair, gravel roads and a hint of corn rows popping up in freshly tilled fields.

"Wonder if any of these fields are Troy's," Jaimie called over the noise from the wind.

"No way. Troy uses no-till farming. He would never expose his soil like this."

"What do you mean?" Jaimie creased her eyebrows, glancing around at the beautiful fertile fields.

"It's a way of drilling the seeds right into the ground without turning the soil over," Melissa explained. "The no-till drill cuts right into last-year's debris and puts the seed in place without exposing the topsoil. That's how we met."

"Huh?"

"He snapped a roller chain on a broken piece of

glass and came into the store for a new one." Melissa saw an example up ahead. She pointed. "That's what I'm talking about! See how the corn stalks from last year have been cut down but not pulled out of the ground? It holds the soil in place so it can't blow away in the wind."

"That's really cool," Jaimie said. They watched as a family got out of their car and walked toward an old farmhouse. The two little girls and one little boy ran ahead, and their mom and dad lagged behind, holding hands and walking more slowly. The girls and the mom wore homemade dresses and white caps on their heads. "I once asked a Mennonite woman what the cap symbolized."

"What did she say?" Melissa kept her eyes on the family as they passed, even turning almost completely around in her seat to watch them for another few minutes. They were fascinating.

"She said the cap was to symbolize her submissiveness to God and to her husband."

"What?" Melissa turned to her cousin, and her mouth dropped open. "I can understand being submissive to God, but men and women are created equal." She shook her head in disdain.

"Actually, you're wrong." Jaimie corrected her. "Men can't have babies."

"Ooh, you're so right, sista!" Melissa gave her cousin a little fist bump. "Girl power."

"Girl power!" Jaimie shouted out the window. They were far enough away from the farmhouse that there was no way the family could have heard them, but Jaimie gunned the engine, speeding away. Melissa stuck her head out the passenger-side window, whooping like a cowgirl.

They eventually wandered back to civilization and felt high on life as they headed home. When they pulled in to Jaimie's driveway, Melissa folded down the vanity mirror and tried to pat her windblown hair down and pull it into a ponytail holder. Her hair felt like coarse straw. She shook her head at the lost cause and instead smiled at her own fiery green eyes in the reflection.

"Girl power," she whispered, shut the mirror, and walked into the house.

Chapter Six—Startling Revelations

"My lady…" Troy held the passenger door of his truck for her, and Melissa climbed up into luxury. She touched the leather seats and gaped at the state-of-the-art sound system, powerful speakers, and wood trim. When Troy came around to the driver's side and clicked his seat belt into place, she raised her eyebrows at him.

"What'd you do? Get the fully-loaded version?"

"What?" Troy's purposely innocent face revealed a sheepish grin. "It's a working truck. Don't you like it?"

"Yeah, right. Working truck. Humph." She shook her head and grinned at him.

"How was your weekend?" Troy casually took her hand from where it rested on the seat. Her breath sped up. His hand was strong and masculine. She tried to pull herself together so she could answer him.

"Oh, you know. Worked all day Saturday, church on Sunday." She spoke dismissively, as if she hadn't spent the whole previous afternoon roaming the countryside trying to figure out which farm was his. "You?"

"About the same." He winked at her. It didn't take more than a few minutes to pull into the parking lot of the little restaurant. He came around to help her out of the truck. When her feet hit the ground, he kept his hands on her hips for just a little longer than he needed to and looked down into her eyes.

Her heart raced, and she almost thought he was going to lean down and kiss her. Instead, he made a little sound in the back of his throat, took her hand and led her through the parking lot toward the entrance. He paused and looked at her nervously.

"Now, just remember. Everybody knows me. It's a small town, and you are new and exciting. People are going to stare and gawk. You're kind of like… a celebrity. Don't let it go to your head *too much*."

"It sounds like maybe you need to try not to let it go to *your* head too much." She bumped her shoulder into his arm playfully. "I mean, you *are* holding the hand of a celebrity."

"Maybe it's you who is holding the hand of a celebrity, and you just don't know it yet." He paused again, and the piercing intensity of his eyes bore into her.

She saw that hunger in his eyes again. She gulped and felt as if she couldn't breathe. She wished he would just kiss her already and get it over with, but again, he pulled away slightly and gripped her hand a little tighter. Something shifted in his expression. *He's nervous. Why?*

Troy took a deep breath, let it out, and led her toward the door. When Melissa entered the small dining room, not many people paid her much attention. Until Troy stepped up beside her. Then some people did a double take, leaned over, and whispered to the person across the table, and that person would turn around as well. It made her extremely uncomfortable, but she reminded herself that he had warned her ahead of time.

The case of cookies and pies pulled her attention to her right, and her mouth started watering. The smell of freshly baked bread overpowered her senses, and she almost moaned. Her stomach growled, and she was tempted to skip lunch and head straight over to the case of delicacies. Someone clearing his throat drew her attention back.

A man with a hardened expression stepped up to the host stand and picked up two menus. His monogrammed shirt read *Patrick*, and Melissa got the impression that he was the owner of the restaurant.

"Troy…" He spoke through clenched teeth, then turned a forced smile to Melissa. "Will it be just the two of you?"

"Yes, Uncle Patrick," Troy replied. He rested his hand lightly on Melissa's lower back. "I'd like you to meet Melissa Dalton. She just moved into town."

Melissa could almost hear the warning in his voice telling his uncle that he'd best make her feel welcome. She raised her eyebrows at Troy and mouthed the word "Uncle?" He just winked at her and turned back to his uncle Patrick.

He spun on his heel and started walking toward the back of the dining room. Melissa took that as a cue that she should follow, and Troy gestured for her to lead the way. He kept his hand protectively on her lower back, and she might have felt comforted by it if it weren't for the stares coming from all around her. She confidently held her head high and followed Patrick to where he was laying placemats and menus on the table.

Troy held her chair for her, but as she sat down, he suddenly stiffened and stepped over to his uncle. He spoke quietly and firmly and sounded almost angry. "When did Becca start waitressing here?"

"Last week, why?"

"Why didn't anyone tell me? I wouldn't have brought her here." Troy and Patrick both glanced her way and Melissa felt her stomach drop. "Don't you dare give her to us as a waitress."

Uncle Patrick held up a little card that was already in his hand, with a name written on it in flowing, feminine handwriting. The name of their intended waitress. He set it down on the table, and Melissa read the name... Becca.

"She's the only waitress who is not already over-sat. You're a big boy. You can handle it." With that, Patrick turned and stomped away.

"You've *got* to be kidding me," Troy mumbled under his breath, almost too quietly for Melissa to hear. He slowly walked around the table, pulled out his chair, and sat down hard. He lowered his gaze and gripped his hair.

"Ex-girlfriend?" Melissa guessed. Troy looked up with vitriol in his eyes.

"We were never a couple," he insisted. "We have never been a couple, we will never be a couple, and it is not my fault that she clings to the childish notion that we ever will be."

"Gee, tell me how you really feel, Troy." Melissa pulled his hand from his hair and brushed the disheveled locks into place but kept his hand resting in hers. She squeezed his hand gently and smiled lightly.

"How do you do that?" Troy whispered.

"How do I do what?"

"Calm me down like that." His eyes were soft, almost in awe.

"Guess I just have a soothing touch." She brushed her thumb across the back of his hand and raised her eyebrows. He raised his right back at her. Her breathing sped up at the suggestive nature of their non-verbal conversation.

Melissa felt a presence at her left elbow. Troy's hand quickly released hers, and he picked up the menu that rested on the table. Knowing he probably had the menu memorized, Melissa guessed correctly that the young lady standing beside her was Becca.

Melissa looked up to see a beautiful girl with big brown eyes, a handsewn dress and apron, hair tucked up in a delicate twist, and the traditional Mennonite cap on her head.

Oh my gosh. Melissa felt her stomach plummet, and she turned back to Troy. His eyes were nervous, almost apologetic. She raised her chin slightly and looked up at Becca.

Becca's eyes bore into her with disdain, but she spoke in the sweetest fake enthusiasm she could muster through clenched teeth. "I *know* what Troy wants, but what can I get *you* to drink... Melissa?"

"Nice to meet you, too, Becca." Melissa spoke just as curtly back. "I'd like a Diet Coke." Becca didn't even look at Troy, didn't write anything down, just turned and walked quickly away.

Melissa watched Becca leave, then took a moment to glance around the dining room. Many people were still staring, some were trying to pretend they weren't, and some patrons were oblivious. As she looked around, it was clear that every waitress in the building was dressed in traditional Mennonite clothing, as were about a third of the patrons in the dining room. Many of the men wore the same neatly trimmed beard as Troy's.

Some patrons looked like businessmen and women from the local stores and offices. Melissa would have fit right in with them. Those people were mostly ignoring her. It was as if they had no idea there was a scandal brewing. The Mennonites were staring at her like a cockroach that needed to be exterminated... immediately.

Melissa turned back to Troy and tucked both hands in her lap. She took a deep breath and looked him in the eye. He still hadn't spoken and wasn't smiling. Puzzle pieces she didn't even know were missing fell into place, completing a picture she wasn't sure she could hang on her wall. The location of his farm, his neatly trimmed beard, the fact that he'd never been on a date, his old-fashioned speech and cadence.

Her whisper was little more than a breath. "You're a *Mennonite.*"

41

Chapter Seven—Pot Roast

"A Mormon girl and a Mennonite guy," Troy whispered. He sat back in his chair and put his hands behind his head. "What an interesting combination."

"How'd you know I was Mormon?" Melissa pursed her lips.

"Apparently I'm better at doing research than you are."

"I hadn't realized I needed to make a trip to the library in order to go on a date," she said.

The tension in the air was almost palpable when Becca came back with their drinks. Melissa had her arms crossed and Troy still had his hands behind his head. Neither of them broke eye contact long enough to give Becca any acknowledgment that they were ready to order. She stood with her little notebook in her hand, pencil ready, and cleared her throat.

"Becca, can I ask you a question?" Melissa smirked at Troy to watch for his reaction.

"Uh… sure."

"How long have you known Troy?" They still didn't break eye contact.

"As long as I can remember, why?"

"Would you say he's a good man?" Melissa saw him shake his head almost imperceptibly.

"Why are you doing this?" Troy whispered. Melissa ignored him.

"Should I be in any way concerned to be alone with him, like for instance if he asked me out on a date?" Melissa already knew the answer to her rhetorical question, so she continued. "Would you think that it would be necessary to… research his background before going out with him?"

"Uh…" Becca stammered. Melissa finally broke eye contact and smiled sweetly up at Becca.

"Would you want him to research *your* background before he took *you* out on a date?"

Becca barely glanced at Melissa before meeting Troy's piercing eyes. Something passed between the childhood friends, and Becca seemed to take a half step back.

"If I had to make an educated guess right now…" She almost sounded as if she was choking back tears. "I'd guess… that I will never get the chance to find out." With that, she ran from the room.

"Was this your way of showing me your religion without having to tell me? By bringing me here?" Melissa asked.

"When were you planning to tell me that you're Mormon?" Troy leaned forward and forced her to look him in the eye.

"Why does that matter?" She barely squeaked out

her question.

"Are you ever planning to leave your faith?"

"Of course not."

"Well, neither am I." With finality, he sat back in his chair and took a deep breath.

"Then why are we even sitting at the same table?" Melissa whispered. She felt a tear fall down the side of her face, but she ignored it. If she wiped her cheek, everyone in the restaurant would know she was crying. She had no intention of letting any of them have that satisfaction.

"Because I think I'm in love with you," Troy whispered back. The hardness had yet to leave his eyes, but his words were soft and pure.

"What?" Melissa's breath caught in her throat. "You barely know me…"

"And you're in love with me, too."

Melissa stood up suddenly and tried to calm her breathing. "I… I need to use the ladies' room. Excuse me." She turned around and ran right into Troy's uncle Patrick.

"Going somewhere?"

"Could you point me to the ladies' room, please?" She choked out. He pointed to the hallway by the kitchen. She casually tossed her long hair off the side of her shoulder, letting the curls fall down her back, held her head confidently, and strode over to the hallway, never looking back.

Melissa opened the door to the ladies' room so hard that it crashed into the side wall, causing the crying girl sitting on the floor to jump and look up from where her head was tucked into her arms. "Becca? What are you doing in here?"

"Getting away from Troy." There was almost an underlying *obviously* at the end of Becca's statement.

"What a coincidence..." Melissa sighed and then sat down hard on the floor next to the girl who probably woke up that morning thinking she was someday going to marry Troy Weller. They sat in silence for a few moments. Finally, Melissa looked over at Becca and frowned slightly. "He just told me he's in love with me."

"Well, he just all but told me that he's *not* in love with me." They both sighed at the same time and chuckled at each other.

"What are we supposed to do now?"

"I guess I need to shake off the childish fantasies I've clung to all these years and get on with my life." Becca tucked her knees to her chest tighter and rested her chin on them.

"I guess I'm gonna need to figure out how to tell my Mormon parents that I'm in love with a Mennonite guy."

"I don't even know what a Mormon is," Becca said.

"Well, I know very little about the Mennonite faith too." Melissa tugged lightly at one of the white strings hanging down from Becca's cap. Becca tugged lightly at one of Melissa's long strawberry blonde curls.

"Maybe we can teach each other."

"That sounds good," Melissa replied. "You know what else sounds good?"

"What?"

"Your pot roast here. I heard it's delicious." She smiled over at Becca.

"It is," Becca acknowledged.

"I could use a good waitress to bring me a plate of it." She raised her eyebrows. "I tip well."

"You had *better* make Troy pay for your lunch, or I'm going to smack him upside the head." They both chuckled, and Melissa stood and brushed herself off, then reached down to offer Becca a hand.

As they walked out of the ladies' room arm in arm, Melissa whispered over to Becca, "I guess I need to reconcile with my new boyfriend before he finds some other girl to take to lunch."

"Wonder what religion she'll be…" They giggled and ignored the stares from all the tables nearby.

Melissa enjoyed the confusion and fear in Troy's eyes as she slid into the seat across from him. Becca smiled at him peacefully.

"You want the pot roast too, Troy? Or do you need some more time to *decide*?"

"Thank you, Becca," Troy said, a soft smile playing across his face. Although he answered Becca, his eyes never left Melissa's. "I think I *have* decided that I would like the pot roast."

He reached cautiously across the table and opened his hand, inviting Melissa to meet him halfway. She smiled back at him and laid her small hand inside his, allowing his strength to flow through her.

Becca chuckled and walked away.

Chapter Eight—Confessions

Conversation at lunch had been understandably strained, and Melissa got the impression they would discuss their confusing predicament at a later date and time.

"I have a confession to make," Troy said. He offered his hand to help Melissa up into the passenger side of his truck.

Troy stood beside the truck and held on to the door frame, tucking his fingers into the crease there. He leaned slightly forward, allowing his arms to support his weight. His face was close to hers but not too close. His light brown eyes pierced into hers as he took a deep breath and let it out slowly.

"I've never kissed a girl before."

Wow, okay. So he'd been serious about never having dated prior to her. That's not such a bad thing. Melissa touched his cheek. He leaned his face into her hand and closed his eyes.

"Why are you telling me this now?" she asked.

He opened his eyes. "I just thought you might want to know what you're getting yourself into."

"Probably a little late for that," Melissa whispered.

"You've fallen for me, haven't you?" Troy baited her.

"You already know the answer to that question, and you're a cad for asking me to admit it." She slowly drew her hand away from his face but smiled softly.

"Sorry," he whispered and returned her soft smile.

"You're not even supposed to be alone with me, are you?" Melissa asked.

"No, not really," he admitted. From what little Melissa knew about the Mennonite religion, dating was not allowed. No wonder every Mennonite in that restaurant had looked at Troy as if he was a cockroach bringing a harlot into their midst. They had been just as angry at him as they'd been with her, probably more so.

"So what are you going to do?"

"I'm going to ask my brother and his wife Jessica to have us over for dinner soon so I can spend more time with you... in the company of a chaperone."

"Don't you trust yourself with me?" Melissa realized her voice had taken on a lighthearted flirtation.

He answered by firmly shaking his head back and forth emphatically. "No, ma'am, I do not."

They both chuckled, breaking the seriousness of the situation.

"And I need to meet your father as soon as possible."

"My father?" She raised her eyebrows.

"Yes, I will not disrespect him by continuing to pursue your affection."

"Do I get to meet your parents?"

Troy gulped. "Of course."

"They're not going to like me, are they?" Melissa wondered if meeting his parents would be like an intensified version of how things played out in the restaurant.

"They'll grow to love you," Troy said. "Just like I do."

"It's too soon for you to love me."

"I don't believe that." He brought her hand to his chest, positioning her palm over his heart. "When it's right, you can feel it. In here. Piercing you to your core."

"In a romance novel, they would call that insta-love," she teased, not pulling her hand away.

"I've never read a romance novel," Troy said, keeping his hand over hers. "I just know what I read in your emerald eyes."

"What do you read in my emerald eyes?" she whispered.

"That you're the woman God made for me," he whispered back. "And I'm the man God made for you."

"That was very nice of him," she said.

"I need to spend some time in prayer and consecration," Troy said. "And prepare myself to be worthy of you."

"You'd better take me back to work, then." Melissa told him, wishing she could pull him down for a first kiss but sensing that her first kiss from him would be at the altar, should they continue this trajectory. She had a strong suspicion that was exactly where they were heading.

Troy raised her hand to his cheek again and held it there. His eyes closed for a few seconds, and he seemed to breathe in the scent of her wrist.

It was quite possibly the most romantic moment of Melissa's life.

Troy finally released her hand from his face but held it gently in his for a moment more and looked into her eyes. He squeezed her hand, placed it on her leg, then stepped away from her. He closed the truck door, walked around, and climbed into the driver's side.

Neither of them spoke during the drive back to the store, and they never touched again, even as he held the car door to let her out at the entrance to the Farm and Tractor Supply store. One final longing gaze into her eyes, then he climbed into his truck and drove away.

Chapter Nine—What's Your Next Move?

"I don't want you to leave us alone or anything; I just don't want you to… listen." Troy smiled sheepishly.

"Listen to what?" Craig asked, then held up his hands and backed up slightly. "Wait, you are *not* proposing to that girl! You barely know her."

"Of course not…" Troy scuffed his boot into the gravel and kicked a large stone at the side of the driveway. "I want to… try to… kiss her."

"You're not supposed to be kissing her before you marry her," Craig scolded. "You know the rules. Why do you want to be such a rebel?"

"You telling me you didn't kiss Jessica before you got married?"

"That is none of your business…"

"Yeah, see. You act all high and mighty like you're this perfect saint and I'm a heathen for even wanting to try to kiss my sweetheart." Troy poked his brother in his side, forcing him to smile. "Besides, you tell me I can't marry her… yet. Then you tell me I can't kiss her until we're married. How fair is that?"

"Have Dad and Mom even met her?" Craig raised his eyebrows, then wrapped his arm around Troy's shoulders, and dragged him up the stairs to the front porch. "Have you met her parents?"

"Her parents live up near Saginaw somewhere," Troy said. "But, no. I haven't brought her over to meet Mom and Dad yet. One step at a time, right? I haven't even seen her since Monday."

"Ooh, you've gone a whole day and a half without being near her? I'm impressed." He opened the door and called to Jessica. A little blond boy toddled into the hallway, wearing only a diaper and dragging his bath towel.

"Grab him, will you?" Jessica called. "I can't get him to sit still long enough to get these clothes on him."

The brothers came around the corner to see a very disheveled-looking woman on the floor in the bathroom, covered up to her elbows in bath water, muddy toddler clothes strewn everywhere, and mud covering every wall of the tub. Jessica looked up at them and sighed.

"He heard you guys coming up the stairs, and he just squirmed out my arms."

"How about if I help him get dressed," Troy suggested, scooping his nephew into his arms. "Craig can clean up the bathroom, and you can go… change into something… dry."

"What time are Melissa and her cousin going to be here?" Jessica pushed herself off the floor. "I need to finish getting dinner ready."

"About twenty minutes," Troy called as he was walking toward his nephew's bedroom. He started tickling baby Jesse and shoving arms into sleeves. "You hold still for Uncle Troy now. You hear me?" It took almost half of those twenty minutes to wrestle the little guy into his clothes, but Troy was less nervous afterward.

"Tell me again what she's like," Jessica called from the kitchen. Troy walked in and was amazed at how quickly she had been able to pull herself together. She had changed into a clean dress, straightened her disheveled bun and replaced the cap on her head, and was calmly pulling a casserole dish from the oven as if she hadn't just been up to her elbows in bathwater ten minutes prior. "Becca said she was really sweet."

"Can we not talk about Becca tonight?" Troy leaned against the counter and lifted one corner of a cloth to reveal a plate of brownies.

"Get out of there!" Jessica slapped Troy's hand away. "Those are for after dinner. Tell me about Melissa."

"She's…" Troy felt his eyes glaze over, and he sighed. "She's feisty."

"Feisty?"

"Headstrong, confident, passionate… the most amazing emerald eyes."

"I heard she's beautiful." Jessica raised her eyebrows. "From… like… everyone."

"That's what people keep telling me, but she's so much more than that. I don't even know how to describe it."

"Oh, you have fallen hard for this girl, haven't you?"

"More than I want to admit…" Just then there was a knock on the door, and Troy jumped from where he was leaning against the counter. "She's here!"

Jessica shook her head and grabbed the kitchen towel from the rack by the stove as she pushed past him. "I'll get the door."

Craig beat her to it. He and baby Jesse were already greeting their guests, and Melissa's cousin was cooing over the baby, taking him in her arms. Troy met Melissa's eyes, and it seemed there was no one else in the hallway. An invisible force pulled him forward, and before he realized he'd walked down the hall, his hand was laced with hers and her soft smile reached all the way into his soul.

"Ms. Dalton, so good of you to come," Troy whispered.

"Mr. Weller, thank you for having me over." Melissa squeezed his hand just slightly.

"Hey," Jessica barged into the conversation. "It's my house you're visiting. Troy can gaze into your eyes for the rest of his life. It's my turn to get to know you."

Jessica broke up the handholding and pulled Melissa away toward the kitchen. Melissa glanced longingly back at Troy and shrugged in mock defeat. Troy leaned against the wall in the hallway and watched her walk away. He listened as Melissa complimented Jessica on how wonderful the freshly baked bread smelled and how lovely her kitchen was.

Yeah, he'd admit it. He was falling hard for Melissa. What was he going to do now? He refused to leave the

Brethren, she refused to leave her faith. Both of their denominations expected young people to marry within their church. Yet here they stood, falling in love.

"What's your next move, little brother?" Craig leaned against the wall in the hallway, where they could hear his wife talking with Melissa, getting along like kindred spirits.

"Want to take a drive with me up to Saginaw?" Troy asked his wise older brother. "I think I need to introduce myself to Mr. Dalton."

Chapter Ten—Temptations

"Would you like to take a walk with me?" Troy asked Melissa before they settled into the living room after dinner. "There's something I want to show you out behind Jessica's garden."

"You are *not* taking her over there," Craig warned.

"I won't. Geesh. I just want to show her."

"Humph."

"Show me what?" Melissa asked, an excited lilt to her voice.

"You'll see." As soon as they were around the corner into the hallway, Troy lifted her hand and intertwined their fingers. Knowing hand holding was about as far as he should take his physical contact with her prior to marriage, he was embarrassed by the conversation he'd had with his brother about wanting to kiss her. Yes, he wanted to kiss her, but Craig had been right. The church was clear on this matter. Troy never understood the reasons behind the commandment until Melissa came into his life. He turned his attention back to her and gave her hand a little squeeze. "How was your day?"

"Nice to have an excuse to leave the store at a decent hour," she said. "Not that I mind staying late. I need to get acquainted with all facets of the store, from opening to closing, if I'm going to be an effective manager."

"You're doing a great job so far." He held open the back door for her to step down into the yard.

"Thank you."

Troy changed the subject and held his arm out in a sweeping gesture, indicating the beautifully tended masterpiece that monopolized most of the half acre this side of the knoll. "This is Jessica's garden."

"It's incredible," Melissa said, walking forward along the cobblestone path. "They must do a lot of canning because there is so much here. Or do they sell the vegetables at a farmer's market?"

"Just Jessica," Troy said. "Craig doesn't work in the garden much."

"I thought he was a farmer." Melissa's brow creased.

"Farming and gardening are not the same thing," Troy explained. "What Craig and I do is mostly riding a tractor and doing repairs and upkeep on the tractors and planters, soil analysis, seed preparation, weed control, harvesting, that kind of thing. Gardening is an art."

"Well, Jessica creates beautiful art."

"Yes, she does," Troy agreed. They came to the end of the garden, where cobblestone steps led to the top of the knoll. Troy held Melissa's hand as they ascended the stairs, watching her face for her reaction when she saw the view for the first time. He wanted to capture this moment in his memory.

"Oh, wow." Melissa's face glowed with wonderment, and Troy understood why. The rolling hills between Craig's property and Troy's were breathtaking. The hills were sometimes frustrating to plant and harvest, and the low-lying areas often flooded in the spring, but the view was awe-inspiring.

"See that little house over on that hill?" Troy pointed across the field to where his home was nearly complete. "That's the home I'm building where I can raise my family." His voice had lowered to a reverent declaration of love. He released Melissa's hand and wrapped his arm around her waist.

Melissa surprised him by wrapping both of her arms around his waist. Troy could understand why this was a bad idea and knew he needed to pull away. One stolen moment with her body against his, and then he wouldn't allow himself this much temptation again until their wedding night.

"I purposely built the house on top of the hill rather than on the protected side of the hill because I wanted to be able to look out the windows and see this." He gestured his arm wide, showcasing the beauty of the landscape, then turned himself toward Melissa and looked down into her eyes. "I haven't picked out paint colors for the walls yet. Or carpeting. Or furniture."

The softness of her gaze told him that she understood his message. He was waiting for her. In more ways than one. In all ways physically and emotionally possible.

"I hope my brother is watching us right now," Troy said.

"Why?" Melissa creased her brow.

"Because then he'll know that I resisted the

overwhelming temptation to lean down and kiss you right now."

"Is that against your religious convictions? To kiss me?"

"The first time I kiss you will be when the minister gives me permission to kiss my bride." Troy's voice had grown in intensity and hunger.

"That is the most romantic thing I've ever heard," Melissa whispered.

"And then I'm not going to stop kissing you for a very long time."

They both chuckled and pulled away from one another.

"Anyway, I wanted to show you our home, and the view from the kitchen window." Troy took her hand and turned back toward the cobblestone steps leading down into the garden.

"I'd like to see the view from inside that kitchen window one of these days," she answered, swinging their arms playfully between them. "And maybe some paint swatches."

"And carpet samples?" He lifted her hand to support her carefully down the steep steps.

"I don't know. We should probably have hardwood floors," Melissa said. "I know how much disregard farmers have about taking their shoes off at the door."

"Maybe just carpet in the living room," Troy suggested. "Where we can have a nice, big easy chair where I can sit with you on my lap while we read scriptures together each evening after dinner."

"That sounds heavenly."

"Which? Sitting on my lap? Or reading scriptures together?"

"Both." She wrapped her arms around his waist again when they were almost to the house, and Troy realized he needed to clarify some boundaries.

He stopped her ten feet from the house and pulled back slightly, pulling her arms from around his waist and holding her hands in his. "I need to tell you a couple of things."

"Okay." Her face fell in confusion.

"Reading scriptures together is something we *can* do before we're married. And doing so will help us to keep our minds and hearts focused on Christ as we're preparing to enter the covenants of marriage."

"I would love that, Troy." Her voice was soft as she gazed up at him. He hated to take away any happiness from this moment, but this conversation needed to happen now, or he wouldn't have the strength to resist her later. The more he held her, the more he wanted to hold her.

"This is as close as we can get."

Melissa kind of glanced side to side with a crease on her brow.

"To each other," he clarified. "I should not have wrapped my arms around you, and I should not have allowed your arms to wrap around me. My body is confused and frustrated, and I will spend time this evening, on my knees, repenting of the carnal thoughts I've had about your body today."

"Troy, isn't that kind of extreme?" She gulped.

"Matthew 5:28 teaches that whosoever looketh upon a woman to lust after her hath committed adultery with her in his heart," Troy said. "I have definitely lusted after you. And I need to stop."

"Okay." Her voice was nearly a squeak, and her eyes sparkled with unshed tears. "I won't wrap my arms around you again."

"And I won't wrap my arms around you again," he promised.

"I'll try," they said at the same time and then chuckled.

That was the moment Craig opened the back door with a stern but compassionate expression. "Jessica has dessert ready."

"Brownies," Troy told Melissa, giving her hands a little squeeze.

"I love brownies." Melissa turned toward the house and Craig held the door open for them.

After she had stepped inside, Craig placed his arm on Troy's shoulder and looked him in the eye. His whisper was sincere. "I'm proud of you."

With that one statement, Troy knew that his older brother had indeed been watching from the house the whole time they'd been standing on the hill. Troy nodded with conviction. "I'm proud of myself too."

Chapter Eleven—What Kind of Plants are You Growing Down There?

"Mr. Dalton," Troy spoke confidently into the phone. "I'm in love with your daughter, and I'd like to come meet you, sir."

"Pardon me?" The voice on the other end of the phone sounded as confused as Troy expected. "Who is this?"

"My name is Troy Weller, sir." Troy coughed lightly, suddenly more nervous than he had been while tapping numbers into his phone. "I met Melissa here in Lowell where she works, but I understand you live up near Saginaw, so I figured I'd better call first before showing up at your door unexpectedly."

"Uh… she's been there three weeks."

"I know that, sir. I'm sorry it's taken me this long to call you. It's supposed to rain tomorrow, so I won't be able to get out in the field, and I figured you would be free as well. I felt it was best if I came to meet you as soon as possible. What time would be agreeable for you?"

"T-tomorrow?" Mr. Dalton sounded almost angry. "Is this a joke? Are you on drugs, son? What kind of plants are you growing down there?"

"Well, my current rotation is corn and soybeans, but I always plant cover crops with alfalfa and some radish before harvest, and of course I farm mostly no-till with some mulch-till every couple of years. I try to take care of my soil, sir."

"That's not what I meant…" Mr. Dalton hesitated, then sighed. "How many acres you got, son?"

"A hundred and eighty, sir. But some of it's wet and swampy, so I've set that aside for wildlife and left some wooded. I only plant about a hundred and sixty."

"Got livestock?"

"Not like you do, sir," Troy said. "Just a few chickens in my yard. But I buy my beef from a very reputable organic farmer down by Clarkesville."

"And you like my daughter?"

"No sir, I *love* your daughter."

"How could you possibly love her this quickly?" Mr. Dalton asked.

"Well, my father always told me that love is a choice, and once he found a wife for me, I'd learn to love her. But with Melissa, it was like God chose her for me instead. We may run into a couple of snags along the way, but I know we can push through them and choose to make this work." Troy felt as if he was talking too fast, so he stopped and waited for Mr. Dalton to respond.

"I don't know what to do about this…"

"Well, perhaps if I come meet you and shake your hand and look you in the eye, you can decide if I'm an acceptable man for your daughter."

"Sounds like that's… probably a good idea," Mr. Dalton said.

"How early can I come meet you, sir?"

"Is Melissa coming with you?"

"Of course," Troy said. "And my brother and his wife and their baby. I would never presume to travel that far without a chaperone, I promise."

"A chaperone?"

"Yes, sir."

"Well, how's late morning sound?" Mr. Dalton asked. "I'll have my wife make us some lunch."

"That sounds wonderful, sir," Troy said. "I look forward to meeting you."

Chapter Twelve—We Are Very Different

Pulling up to Melissa's parents' modest farmhouse had Troy's stomach dancing with butterflies. What were her parents going to think? They probably already thought he was nuts for his old-fashioned way of requesting an audience with her father.

The rain had let up as they'd driven east, and now a light haze hung over the freshly planted fields around the perimeter of the Dalton's feedlot. Theirs was a decent-sized livestock operation, commercial but not industrial.

Troy pulled his truck around the circle drive and parked close to the front door, with the passenger side toward the house so that the women wouldn't have to walk as far. He hurried around the front of the truck to hold open the door for Melissa as Craig helped unclip baby Jesse from his car seat harness before walking around to hold open the door for his wife.

Melissa's mother stepped out the front door and smiled down at them from the porch. Her eyes met his, and he returned her smile, lacing his fingers through Melissa's and trying to calm his nerves.

Because he was watching Melissa's mom so intently, Troy knew the minute her mom saw Jessica climb down from the truck, because her smile faltered, and her lips pursed. That didn't take long. She'd pieced the puzzle together even more quickly than Melissa. With a forced smile and hardened eyes, Mrs. Dalton stepped off the porch and approached her daughter.

"Mom, this is my friend Jessica, her husband, Craig, and their adorable baby, Jesse." Then Melissa pulled him closer and said with pride in her voice. "And *this* is Troy."

"Pleasure to meet you, Mrs. Dalton." Troy offered his hand. "Thank you for allowing us to come meet you and your husband."

She hesitated a second or two longer than was socially acceptable, and Troy wondered if she was going to leave him hanging. Finally, she clasped his hand with the firm, calloused grip of a farmer's wife. She didn't respond with words, just looked at her daughter with raised eyebrows.

"Where's Daddy?" Melissa asked, glancing toward the barn.

"I'm right here." A gruff voice pulled Troy's attention back to the front door, where an intimidating man stepped onto the porch, his hardened expression an outward display of his disappointment at seeing the man holding his daughter's hand.

Troy made a split-second decision to drop Melissa's hand and approach her father with a confident stride and an outstretched hand. "Mr. Dalton, my name is Troy Weller. I'm honored to meet you, sir."

"Melissa, you didn't tell me your friend was

Amish." Mr. Dalton didn't reach for Troy's hand.

"Mennonite, actually, sir," Troy said, clearing his throat and not lowering his hand.

Mr. Dalton looked Troy up and down with disdain, and Troy wondered if this was how Melissa had felt when he'd brought her to his uncle's restaurant. Perhaps they both should have been more upfront with their families and friends.

Perhaps their families and friends should be more accepting of their choice in life partners.

The teachings of his youth came pouring into his heart. *You will be excommunicated if you marry outside the church.*

Troy wondered if this was the case with Melissa's faith as well. Would she be excommunicated from her church if she marries him? Was he taking away her fellowship with her friends and family if he took her away and kept her for himself? He dropped his hand and lowered his gaze. No wonder their families were upset if that was what they all believed.

Melissa rushed to his side and wrapped her arms around his waist. Troy forgot his promise to keep his body away from hers as he pulled her close. This was different. There was nothing sexual in nature with this embrace. This was his future wife clinging to him for comfort and support, and he was man enough to provide that for her.

Craig stepped forward. "Perhaps we should return home. If we're not welcome here..."

"No," Troy insisted. "This good man and woman are Melissa's parents, and I will not leave until I have shown them the proper respect due to them."

"Of course, we don't want you to leave." Melissa's mom stepped forward. "Your religious preferences just took us by surprise, that's all."

"Are you going to force our daughter to dress in homemade clothes and cover her head whenever she's out in public?" Mr. Dalton asked Troy but pointed to Jessica as if she were dressed in rags instead of a modest and quality piece of clothing she'd spent hours crafting.

"Mr. Dalton, I think you misunderstand our religion, sir. The devotional head covering is scriptural based, right out of the Bible, and should only be worn by a woman who is truly converted to the Lord's will."

"Are you saying my daughter is not following the teachings of Christ if she doesn't put a little cap on her head?" Melissa's father narrowed his eyes at Troy. This wasn't going well.

"I'm saying that Jessica is wearing that cap on her head as an outward symbol of her devotion to Christ and to her husband."

"You mean her submission to her husband."

"We submit to the will of the Lord in all that we do, sir," Troy said with confidence. "Just as Christ submitted to the Father, men are provided to women as their protector and women are provided to men as a helpmeet."

"Men and women are created equal," Mr. Dalton insisted.

"I beg to differ, sir. I may not be married, and I may not have seen a woman without clothing, but I know enough about men's and women's bodies to know that we are very different."

"That's not what I meant."

"God made us different on purpose," Troy said. "He made us this way so that we can bring forth children and raise them unto him."

"And you think women should stay home and raise babies and do the housework and cook you dinner?" Mr. Dalton asked.

"Who else would you have nurse your grand babies? Would you prefer we hire someone to do that?" Troy lifted his chin.

"Did you get my daughter pregnant?" Her father took a step toward him, but Troy didn't back down.

"How could I get her pregnant when I have never even kissed her? I've never been alone with her. I will not take her to our marriage bed until we are married."

"I'm never giving you permission to marry my daughter." His words were definitive.

"Then I think our visit has concluded." Troy's heart fell at the realization. "At least now I know where you stand."

"Wait, I made lunch," Mrs. Dalton said. "You must be hungry. Can't you stay for a little while? I want to see my daughter."

"The spirit of contention is not becoming to those who follow Christ," Troy said. "I know when I'm not wanted."

"I want you," Melissa said. "I don't care what my parents say."

Melissa's mother gasped. Troy didn't blame her.

"Well, I do care," Troy said. "You belong to your mother and father until at which time they choose to give you to a man to be his wife. I will not go against their wishes."

"I don't belong to anyone," Melissa said, pulling her arms from around his waist. "Nor will I ever."

"I'm truly sorry to hear that," Troy said, wishing he could pull her close again. "I would have loved to have you as my wife. But not if I cannot obtain your parents' permission."

"What are you saying Troy? That you're breaking up with me?"

"I don't know what I'm saying, Melissa. I don't know what to think about this. I'm confused, and I need a few minutes alone." Troy took a step backward, then looked around the small circle of family. "If you all want to go inside and have a bite to eat, please do. I'm sure whatever Melissa's mother cooked for you will be much better than a fast-food restaurant on the way home. I'll go for a walk and ponder some things while you're eating."

"How about you and I take a walk together?" Mr.

Dalton suggested. "I'll show you my livestock barn."

"I'd like that, sir. Thank you." Troy lifted his chin with confidence and felt hope for the first time since they'd met.

Chapter Thirteen—Excommunicated

"Thank you for lunch, Mrs. Dalton," Jessica said. "This is lovely."

"You're welcome, Jessica." She set a plate of sandwiches on the table beside a large pitcher of lemonade and a fruit salad. "You can call me Jan."

Melissa wanted to feel hope that everything would work out but had a sinking dread in her heart. All she could think about was the conversation her father and Troy were having in the barn. She wasn't confident they would come to any sort of common ground. Troy was too willing to back down from confrontation, and her father was just bullheaded enough to take advantage of that.

"Relax, Melissa," her mom said, laying a hand on her shoulder. "Things will work out for the best."

"I'm not so sure your definition and ours are the same with that respect," Craig said. "I've been trying to warn Troy since the day he met Melissa that he was playing with fire."

"Well, I'm certainly not going to burn him if that's what you're implying." Melissa folded her arms and lifted her chin.

"I don't think you understand the severity of Troy's predicament. Whatever transpires between him and your father is irrelevant."

"Why?" Her mother sat at the table across from Craig. "Because my husband won't give his permission? Or because Melissa will never submit to being looked at as someone's property?"

"Because Troy will be excommunicated if he marries your daughter."

Melissa and her mother both gasped. They looked at one another with wide eyes, then Melissa turned to Craig. "Isn't that a little extreme?"

"That is a serious departure from sound doctrine," Craig said. "If Troy won't tell you himself, my duty as his older brother is to inform you on his behalf. I never dreamed things would get this far, or I would have told you sooner. If you choose to marry him, you are willfully taking him away from fellowship in his church and his family."

"Are you saying that he would not be welcome among your family if Troy marries Melissa?" her mom asked.

"In certain settings he will be allowed into the gathering." Craig nodded. "In others, he will not."

"I can't do that to him, Momma." Tears filled Melissa's eyes and fell down her cheeks. "I can't take him from his family."

"Maybe it's for the best that you find this out now before you do something rash and end up regretting a marriage that was never meant to be."

"That's a terrible thing to say, Mother." Melissa stood and balled her fists. "I am in love with Troy, and he is in love with me."

"Love is not all that's needed to build a forever marriage," her mom said.

"You're just still mad I didn't marry Andy," Melissa said.

"You were engaged for six months, Melissa. That's hardly enough time to build a foundation for a marriage."

"The fact that we were engaged for six months should be proof that we were not right for one another," Melissa said. "If we'd been meant for one another we would have gotten married right away."

"You are betrothed to someone else?" Craig asked. "And yet you were encouraging my brother?"

"No," Melissa stated emphatically. "We broke off the engagement months ago."

"But your parents made a promise to that man. You are defying your parents' wishes."

"I do not *belong* to my parents," Melissa said through clenched teeth. "And I do not belong to Andy or Troy or you, or anyone else." Melissa ran from the kitchen and stormed up the stairs to her childhood bedroom, throwing herself face down onto her bed and sobbing into her pillow. She felt like a little girl letting her emotions get the better of her.

Not surprisingly, her mother knocked on her door five minutes later and peeked her head in. "Can I come in?"

"Whatever," Melissa said with sarcasm. "You own this house and everything in it, apparently."

"You know that's not true, sweetheart." Her mom sat beside her on the bed. "We've never treated you as if we own you."

"It's true you're disappointed that I'm not marrying Andy." Melissa waited for her mother to respond. Her hesitation spoke louder than her response.

"I just want you to be happy."

Liar, Melissa thought. "I'm happy with Troy."

"Are you happy though, sweetheart? You're crying, he's ready to drive home, your father's upset, his brother's upset. This would never work. You're too different."

"We're not too different," Melissa insisted. "We both love the Lord and want to follow his teachings. Shouldn't that be enough?"

"People don't always interpret the scriptures in the same way," her mom said. "You have to do what's right for you, and Troy has to do what's right for him. Having been married to your father for almost thirty years, I can say with confidence that we're happiest when we're on the same page."

Melissa rolled over and looked up at her mom. "I want to be on the same page with my husband."

Her mother sighed. "I fear you'll have a difficult time staying on the same page if you're reading from a different book."

Her father interrupted from the doorway to Melissa's bedroom. "Troy and his family are waiting by his truck. Would you like to go with them? Or would you rather your mother and I give you a ride home to Lowell?"

"I'll ride home with them." Melissa scooted to the edge of her bed and gave her mom a hug. "I love you, Momma. Thanks for the advice." She walked to the door and tucked herself in her father's arms.

He kissed the top of her head. "Your mother and I love you and want what's best for you, Melissa. I hope you know that."

"Thanks, Daddy."

Melissa trudged down the stairs and out the front door.

Troy was waiting by the passenger door, leaning against the side, with his hands in the pockets of his jeans, staring off into the distance where corn was just popping up in the fields beside her parents' feedlot.

The world felt right for that one tiny moment, and Melissa wanted to run down the porch steps, throw herself into his arms, and demand that he marry her today. She wanted to be with Troy forever. The thought occurred to her that if she married Troy, she would only be with him until they died, not forever. And he would be excommunicated. And she would be heartbroken.

Melissa trudged down the stairs and approached the truck. When Troy turned to face her, his façade fell for the briefest of seconds, and she saw the same desire in his eyes that she felt in her own. Then he pulled his face back into a mask and opened the door for her.

He offered his hand to help her up, and she slid into the leather seat as he closed the door and walked around the front of his truck.

Neither of them spoke to one another or Craig and Jessica in the back seat.

After Troy clicked his seat belt into place but before he put the truck in gear, he stated in a quiet tone, "Your father said no."

That was that. Melissa turned her face to the window and allowed a few tears to fall down her cheeks. The ride home was quiet.

Chapter Fourteen—Eye Candy

Melissa gasped. Not a face she was expecting to see in Lowell, Michigan at her store. "Andy? What are you doing here?"

He was still as hauntingly handsome as he'd been the day she gave him back the enormous engagement ring he'd purchased with his daddy's money. His clean-cut missionary haircut paired well with his smooth, chiseled jaw, Polo shirt and khakis. "Your mom called."

That traitor! "What did she say to you?" Melissa demanded.

"She told me you were having a hard time and could really use a friend," Andy said, his humble smile sincere. "I felt terrible that I wasn't here for you, so I hopped on the next available flight to Grand Rapids."

"You shouldn't have come here." Melissa shook her head in disbelief, keenly aware that they had an audience of store customers, most of whom probably knew that she and Troy had parted ways the previous week.

After driving home from Saginaw in near silence, Troy had dropped Melissa off at her cousin's house and disappeared down the road. She hadn't heard from him since. She cried every night and had bags under her eyes from lack of sleep. She didn't need Andy showing up to make her feel better. She needed Troy.

Melissa glanced over at the little café in the corner, where younger men had returned in recent days to drink burnt coffee and eat complimentary donuts. Likely, they all hoped she would get over her infatuation with Troy and notice one of them. "Come on, let's go to my office where we can talk in private." She turned and strode to the back of the store, knowing Andy would follow her.

He did.

Melissa propped open the door to her office so Andy wouldn't get the idea that she wanted *that* much privacy with him. "Have a seat." She pointed to the chair opposite her desk.

"Can I have a hug first?" Andy asked, holding open his arms and offering subtly pouting lips. How many times had she kissed those lips? Too many.

"I think we've given each other all the hugs we're ever going to give."

"I have a hard time accepting that." Andy reached for her hand and gently pulled her closer. "I still don't understand what I did that made you want to take a break."

"I never said I wanted to take a break," Melissa told him, ignoring the betrayal she was feeling in her heart because Troy was not the man holding her hand. "I said I wanted to break up. There's a difference."

"When two people love each other enough to promise each other forever, that kind of love doesn't just go away. At least it hasn't for me." Andy pulled Melissa just a little closer and rested his hands on her hips. The way he held her felt so natural, so comfortable, so benign. He still didn't elicit any fire from her middle, any racing heart, any accelerated breathing.

They'd been engaged for six months. They'd dated for five months prior to that. Yes, she'd loved him. She probably still did love him. He apparently still loved her. He loved her enough to drop everything and come to Michigan to comfort her.

Andy always treated her with respect. They never disagreed about anything. Andy could give her every imaginable luxury in the world. His family loved her, and her family loved him.

On paper, Andy was everything Melissa wanted and needed. They read and interpreted the scriptures the same way. Andy held the priesthood. He'd served as a missionary. He had a college education. They'd attended the same college.

They knew each other's secrets. Andy knew what kind of chocolate she wanted on the day before her period. He could go to the grocery store and pick out exactly what kind of pads and tampons she wanted.

He knew her birthday. He knew her parents' birthdays. He was with her the day her grandma died. He had loved her for longer than she knew he existed.

Their babies would be beautiful. Their babies would be raised in the church. They would never have to compromise their values or doctrinal beliefs to be together.

If Melissa married Andy, they could be sealed in the temple for time and all eternity in the new and everlasting covenant of marriage.

The only excuse Melissa could give as to why she couldn't marry Andy was because he said that she was beautiful. No, he said she was eye candy.

Was that such a bad thing?

Melissa had never come right out and told Andy that she'd overheard his conversation with his buddy. He was probably justified in his confusion.

"You called me eye candy," Melissa whispered, lowering her gaze. She was eye level with his strong chest muscles, so well-proportioned inside his stylish shirt. The muscles of his arms had just the right amount of breadth. He was the perfect size. Everything about Andy was perfect.

"What? When?" Andy lifted her chin with his finger, and Melissa raised her gaze to meet his.

"You were talking to your friend, John, and you didn't know I overheard you. I could barely stand to be around you after that. I was so hurt." Tears fell from each of her eyes.

"Sweetheart, I don't remember saying that, but if I did, I'm sorry. It's true that you're beautiful. Any man who can't see that is blind."

"You sound like my mother," Melissa said through her tears.

"Your mother's a smart woman." Andy pulled Melissa closer, and she finally submitted to his embrace, allowing her head to rest on his shoulder.

There was still no spark between her and Andy, even as she wrapped her arms around his waist and held him close. She wished there could be. She knew what passion felt like now and nothing could compare. She just couldn't love Andy as more than a friend, or maybe as a sister.

That's probably not how things looked when Troy came racing around the corner and slid to a stop near the door to her office.

Chapter Fifteen—What Color Are My Eyes?

"Troy, wait!" Melissa called as he stormed away from her office. She disentangled herself from Andy's arms and hurried after Troy, following him down the short hallway and into the main showroom floor.

Dozens of customers seemed to suddenly need to shop in the sporting goods section of the store near her office. She ignored them.

"Troy, stop! Come back here."

He wheeled around to face her. "I just needed to see it for myself that you did indeed have your ex-boyfriend with you in your office. Now I know where I stand."

"Is this the guy your father said you weren't allowed to marry?" Andy asked, coming up behind her. "Is he the reason you left me?"

She spun on Andy. "I did not leave you for Troy. I left you because I didn't want to marry you."

"Wait, is this the guy who only wanted to be with you because you were beautiful?" Troy asked.

Melissa now stood between the man she almost married and the man she wished she could marry. They glared at each other with vitriol in their eyes.

"It's *not* true that I only wanted her because she was

beautiful," Andy insisted. "But it is true that she's beautiful. Every man in this building thinks she's beautiful."

"But she is so much more than her beauty," Troy said in hushed awe.

"I am very aware how much more she is than her beauty," Andy insisted. "I have known her for years. And I've loved her for years. I know the strong independent woman that she is. I want to serve by her side forever."

That was hitting below the belt. Andy knew that if Melissa married Troy, she wouldn't be his equal, and she wouldn't be able to get married in the temple forever. They would only be married until they died, and not for eternity. Mennonites didn't believe that marriage could last forever if a couple was sealed in a temple.

"You deserve to have a temple marriage." Andy turned to her and pleaded with his eyes. "You deserve to be married in the everlasting covenant. You deserve to have your children born in the covenant. You deserve to have a man who will treat you like a princess."

"I don't want to be worshipped," Melissa said. "I want to be loved."

"Love is not the only thing that makes a marriage," Andy said. "You and I have a connection that's eternal."

"We can't even get along for an entire conversation," Melissa pointed out. "We're arguing about whether we're in love."

"I'm not arguing *with* you. I'm fighting *for* you. Because I love you, and I've always loved you, and I will always love you. You have my heart, and you will for eternity. Please, I'll do anything. I'll move here so you can continue working. I can find a job here in Michigan, or I can work remotely. I want to be by your side. I want you to feel the kind of love that we felt at the time that I got down on one knee and gave you that diamond ring."

"Your daddy bought that diamond ring."

"And I'm still paying him back." Andy chuckled.

"That's stupid."

"Giving you that ring was the best choice I ever made."

"Accepting that ring was the worst choice I ever made," Melissa said.

"I can't believe that to be true."

Would Andy never give up? Time to bring out the big guns. Two could play at this game. Melissa squeezed her eyes shut. "Andy, what color are my eyes?"

"What are you talking about Melissa?" Andy sighed. "Why does it matter what color your eyes are?"

"Just tell me. Do you remember what color my eyes are?"

"I think they're hazel, right?"

"You tell me," Melissa said.

"I haven't seen you in forever," Andy said.

"Really?" She kept her eyes shut. "Because you've been standing in my office, looking into my eyes for the past half an hour. Now go for it. Tell me what color my eyes are."

"They're hazel," Andy stated confidently.

"Troy, what color are my eyes?" Melissa continued to stand there, with her eyes closed knowing what his answer would be before he said it out loud.

Troy's voice lowered to a husky, burning undertone, and he almost whispered, "Sometimes they're a dark jade. But when the light hits them just right, they sparkle like emeralds."

"That proves nothing!" Andy said. "All that proves is that he thinks you're beautiful also."

"No, it proves that Troy has looked into my soul." Melissa finally opened her eyes and faced Andy. "Troy knows me on a deeper level than any man has ever known me before. It doesn't matter that Troy and I have differences in opinions about doctrine. It doesn't matter that Troy and I belong to different churches. It doesn't matter that Troy and I are going to disagree about a lot of things. What matters is that Troy and I can't keep our eyes off each other. We can't keep our hands off each other. We've never kissed, but I know that once we start kissing, we're never going to want to keep our lips off of each other either."

"I remember a time when you couldn't keep your lips off me either."

"I never felt anything when I kissed you, not the way I feel when I look in Troy's eyes." She turned around and pierced her gaze right into Troy's. "I love you. I can't imagine my life without you. Please come back to me. Please don't shut me out. We can find a way to make everything work. I love you, and I want to be your wife, and I want to serve by your side or behind you or in front of you. Whatever you want. I want to raise your babies, and I want to sleep next to you every night. I want to live beside you for the rest of my life and die in your arms."

Troy didn't hesitate a second beyond Melissa's heartfelt speech. He pulled her into his arms and kissed her with a passion that she never knew possible.

People throughout the store whistled and catcalled and applauded.

Somewhere in Melissa's peripheral vision, Andy took a step back, completely defeated. Maybe now he would head back to Utah and realize their breakup was forever.

When they finally pulled apart to breathe, Troy whispered, "I've wanted to do that since the day I met you."

"Oops," Melissa said with a nervous chuckle. "I guess we didn't wait until our wedding to kiss each other for the first time. You wanted the minister to give you permission to kiss your bride."

"Well, since my minister won't give us permission to get married anyway, it doesn't really matter what he says." Troy chuckled in irony. "I would like to get married civilly right away though because I can't wait to kiss you again."

"I'm totally on board with that plan," she said.

"I know exactly what kind of engagement ring I want to buy you," Troy said with a cocky grin.

"You do?" She bit her lower lip playfully. "What kind?"

"An emerald."

Chapter Sixteen—Once a Cheater, Always a Cheater

"What the heck were you thinking?" Craig yelled the minute they were out of the hardware store. "You just made the biggest mistake of your life."

"I disagree," Troy said, heading toward his truck. When arriving at the Farm and Tractor Supply twenty minutes ago, Troy had slid into the parking lot and created his own space, diagonally and taking up three spots. When he'd gotten several texts from his friends telling him that Melissa's ex-boyfriend was at the store, he'd left the restaurant faster than he could pay for his lunch. Thankfully he and Craig had driven there separately because he left without saying goodbye.

Craig caught up with him before Troy could reach the driver's side of his pickup. "You just kissed a woman to whom you are not married. In public. In front of dozens of people who had cell phones raised, taking pictures and videos of you kissing that woman *in public*."

"You said that twice." Troy ignored his horrible parking job and turned to his brother. "Would you rather have me kiss her in private like you did with Jessica?"

"What I did with Jessica was nothing compared to what you did with Melissa."

"How would anyone ever know?" Troy asked, baiting him. "At least I'm honest in the way I feel about Melissa. My love for her is written all over my face for the world to see. I can't hide my love for her any more than I can hide the nose on my face."

"I'm honest with my feelings about my wife." Craig seemed a little less emboldened now that he'd been called out. "I don't need to make a public fool of myself to show that."

"Yours was an arranged marriage. How do you know whether or not you would have loved each other if you'd met each other and fell in love without having someone tell you that she is the person you should love?"

"Love is a choice," Craig said. "I'm glad that our fathers and the minister recommended that we should marry so that I wasn't blinded by how beautiful Jessica is. And believe me, she's beautiful. I love everything about that beautiful woman."

"Melissa's beautiful too. What's your point?" Troy spun his car keys around his finger.

"I don't lust after my wife the way you lust after Melissa. And I'm glad that she was chosen for me so that I didn't ever have to question whether I was marrying her for the wrong reasons."

"And what are the wrong reasons?" Troy asked, lifting his chin and not liking the direction of this conversation.

"Her looks, her body, the way she gazes into your eyes and sees your *soul*. What does that even mean?"

Craig reached for Troy's right hand and practically flung it in Troy's face. "The way she washes your hands. That's not a reason to love each other. And that's not a reason to marry each other or to build a lifetime foundation. You don't even know that woman. And how could you kiss her when she has betrayed the man to whom she is betrothed?"

"She is no longer engaged to that man." Troy pointed his finger in the direction of the store, knowing Melissa's ex-boyfriend was still inside, presumably saying goodbye forever.

Craig ignored Troy's insistence. "She kissed you right in front of the man she promised to be with for the rest of her life. If she did it to him, she'll do it to you. She's a cheater. And once a cheater, always a cheater."

"She is not a cheater," Troy yelled right back at his brother. "She broke up with him."

"She promised her life to him," Craig said. "There is no stronger bond than that. Divorce is not an option."

"She was never married to him," Troy said. "Just because she promised to get married doesn't mean that she ever was married."

"That's not the way the church will view the situation." Craig shook his head with disgust. "You have defiled her. You have defiled her parents. You have defiled yourself. You have defiled your commitment to the church."

"Good thing I don't claim to be perfect, just like you're not perfect, and Father isn't perfect, and Mother isn't perfect, and Jessica isn't perfect, and Melissa isn't perfect, and no person in our church or her church is perfect." Troy took a moment to calm down, knowing this spirit of contention was proving the validity of his rant. "That's why we have the power of repentance. That's why God sent his son Jesus Christ to be our Redeemer. Because we're not perfect. And we never will be."

"You're just a walking sermon today, aren't you?" Craig sneered. "And after your brazen display of sinful behavior. You shouldn't even be entertaining the thought of marrying that woman."

"I'm not entertaining the thought," Troy said with finality. "I'm planning a wedding."

With that, Troy stomped over to his pickup truck, flung open the door, and spit gravel as he sped out of the parking lot.

Chapter Seventeen

Best View from the House

"This is the best view from anywhere in the house." Troy pulled her gently from the main foyer, dodging stacks of lumber in the nearly finished open living area.

"The kitchen?" Melissa raised her eyebrows playfully, stepping up to the stainless-steel sink with top quality Kohler fixtures. "So that I can enjoy the view while I'm doing dishes?" The sink had been positioned at the corner of the room, with a three-sided window frame providing a panorama of the landscape.

Troy came up behind her and wrapped one arm around her waist and with his other arm pointed out the window to the rolling hills below, where shoots of green plants were just starting to pop up out of the soil. "And if you're lucky, right down there will be a hunk on a tractor slaving in the hot sun to bring home the bacon."

"Those are soybeans, Troy. But good try."

He missed her sarcasm about doing the dishes. In reality, this was the nicest kitchen she'd ever dreamed of owning. Solid surface countertops, glazed tile backsplash, stainless-steel appliances. And he was right. The view was incredible.

"Okay, okay, we'll buy the bacon from your father. I've seen his livestock barn, and he has some of the nicest hogs I've ever seen."

"He does grow some good piggies," she acknowledged, snuggling back into Troy's strong arms, allowing her back to press against his firm chest. "Are you sure you're allowed to hold me like this?"

"I'm definitely not allowed to hold you like this." Troy leaned down and kissed Melissa's neck just over her collar bone. "Which is one of the many reasons I look forward to marrying you. But not yet. I have to show you the rest of the house." He backed away and grabbed her hand playfully, lightening the mood.

She laughed and allowed herself to be pulled along, loving seeing this side of him. In a way she felt as if she'd known Troy for years, even though they'd met just over a month ago. They'd spent so much time getting to know each other those first couple of days before the drama started that their whirlwind romance seemed to have spanned six months.

"They designed the main floor of the house in a way that the kitchen, living room, and home office all walk out onto this wrap around deck." He pulled open the large sliding glass door and led her onto the hardwood deck that had already been sanded and stained a natural finish that blended well with the landscape. "We can put deckchairs all around here so that we can sit and watch the deer in the fields and watch the storms come over the hills and feel the wind in our hair."

This was about as alone as they could get while touring Troy's new home. Contractors throughout the house were still working on finishing touches. There was no privacy. Which was good because they shouldn't be alone. As close as they felt to one another, they would likely fall into each other's arms and kiss until they couldn't see straight. And that needed to wait until their wedding.

Melissa leaned against the railing and gazed out over the rolling hills below. "This is incredible, Troy. How much of this is yours and how much is your brother's?"

"Ours," Troy corrected her, leaning against the railing beside her.

"What?"

"How much of this is *ours?*" Troy said. "You'll need to take ownership of the land because, once we're married, what's mine is yours. We've tried to maintain the continuity of the fields, but you can sort of see where the edge of his property starts based on that tree line over there." He pointed off to the west.

"You know I'm not marrying you for your land and fancy house," she teased, only half joking. They needed to have this conversation. People were already questioning how quickly they'd fallen in love, and thought they were rushing into a marriage that was doomed to failure.

"Why *are* you marrying me?" Troy turned, with a teasing smile, and leaned his hip against the railing so he would have his hands free to pull her closer. He brushed a thick lock of her strawberry blonde hair off her shoulder.

"Because during our first conversation, you told me the names of your chickens."

Troy threw his head back and laughed heartily. "You like chickens, huh?"

"I like the *names* of your chickens," she said, watching his face grow serious again. "Reuben, Simeon, Levi, Judah, Issachar, Zebulun, Joseph, Benjamin, Dan, Naphtali, Gad, and Asher."

"I'm impressed you remembered them in order," he said, then cleared his throat.

"One of my seminary teachers made us memorize the twelve tribes of Israel when we were studying Genesis thirty-five."

"Verses twenty-three through twenty-six," Troy confirmed, meeting her gaze.

"That says something about a man," Melissa said in a low voice. "I could tell that you were more than a cocky farm boy who needed a new roller chain for his no-till drill. You were a man who loved the Lord enough to know God's scriptures so well that you named your chickens after the sons of Jacob."

"They provide me physical nourishment every morning while I sit at the kitchen table reading my spiritual nourishment," Troy said. "How better to honor the service they provide?"

"Don't you think they're going to have gender identity issues if you name them after guys?"

"Nah, they don't mind." Troy brushed off her concern.

"Really? Did they tell you they don't mind?"

"They still give me eggs every morning, don't they?"

"How do you like your eggs cooked?" Melissa asked, adding weight to the question, not just asking how he prepared his own eggs but how he'd like her to cook them for him.

"I usually just crack a bunch of them into a frying pan with some butter and stir until they look done."

Melissa laughed heartily. She could picture him doing just that.

"Why? How do you cook your eggs?" His eyes gleamed.

"I try something a little different each time I cook," she said.

"I'd love to try something different once in a while."

"I'd love to cook you something different every morning." Melissa stepped closer and rested her hands on Troy's arms. "Maybe you could read scriptures to me as I cook eggs."

"I would love to read scriptures to you as you cook eggs laid by *our* chickens who freely roam *our* property and sleep in *our* chicken coop as we sleep upstairs in *our* master bedroom."

"Does our master bedroom have a beautiful view of the rolling hills also?" Melissa asked.

"Heck no." He shook his head with a mischievous grin.

Melissa creased her brow. "Why not?"

"Because I don't plan on having the curtains open while we're in there." Troy pulled her closer and apparently forgot all standards of premarital activities because his lips crushed against hers again, hungry for the chance to get married and take her upstairs to their nearly completed master bedroom and close the curtains.

That was the moment Troy's father stepped onto the deck and growled, "Get your hands off my son."

Chapter Eighteen
You're Not a Mormon?

"Dad, this is Melissa," Troy said, wrapping his arm around Melissa's waist, presenting her to his dad. "Melissa, this is my father, Jonathon Weller."

"It's a pleasure to meet you, Mr. Weller." Melissa stepped forward, with her hand extended. Jonathan didn't take her hand. She wondered if this was how Troy felt meeting her parents.

"What is she doing here?" Jonathon asked, glaring at Troy with wide, angry eyes.

"I was just showing Melissa the home I've commissioned to be built."

"If you were showing her *your* home, why are you outside, with your eyes closed, in each other's arms, kissing?"

Melissa had a difficult time not breaking into laughter. Jonathon had a good point.

"We... uh... got distracted." Troy cleared his throat and glanced at Melissa, who finally lost her resolve and snickered, covering her laugh with a cough.

"This is why you are discouraged from courting," Jonathon stated. "You should not be alone with this woman."

"Dad, our general contractor and about six of his

employees are in various rooms of this house. We are most definitely not alone."

"You shouldn't even be together," Jonathon said.

"Why is that?" Troy folded his arms across his chest and took a protective step in front of Melissa, as if standing between her and the rest of the world, even if that meant standing up to his own father.

"She is not of our faith." Jonathon's statement was definitive, as if that explained everything.

"She is a Christian who loves the Lord, our God. How is that not of our faith?"

"She has not been baptized," Troy's dad said.

"Excuse me, Mr. Weller, but I was baptized when I was eight years old." Melissa lifted her chin in defense. "By a man holding the Aaronic Priesthood."

"Your priesthood is not valid in God's eyes." Jonathon didn't back down.

"Why is that?" Melissa asked.

"You are Mormon," Jonathon said.

"Mormon was a prophet who lived about sixteen hundred years ago," Melissa said. "I am a member of the Church of Jesus Christ of Latter-day Saints."

"What does that mean?" Troy turned to Melissa with confusion in his eyes. "I thought you were a Mormon."

"That's a commonly used misnomer. A nickname if you will. The term actually was originally used in a derogatory way but has come to be more like a badge of honor." Melissa was surprised Troy didn't know this about her religion. "We believe in Jesus Christ. We believe that Christ took upon himself our sins and died on the cross and rose on the third day as a resurrected being. Jesus is my Savior just like he is your Savior."

"Why Mormon?" Troy asked. "If that's not the name of your church?"

"Because we read the Book of Mormon," Melissa said. "It's another testament of Jesus Christ, just like the Bible."

"There is no other scripture besides the Bible," Troy said, taking a step back. He bumped into his father, who seemed vindicated. There was almost an underlying smirk. Troy looked confused. He stammered. "There is... no other... I need a minute."

"Troy." Melissa tried to hurry after him, but Troy's father held up his hand and stood between her and the door.

"I think he's made it clear that he needs a minute." Jonathon folded his arms across his chest.

Chapter Nineteen—Bible Doctrine and the Book of Mormon

"And then he just left, and his dad was standing there all smug and mean and, and, I'm never going to see him again." Melissa grabbed another tissue and cried harder.

"You'll see him again," Jaimie said. "You guys can't stay away from each other." She patted Melissa on the shoulder and pulled her feet up onto the couch. Jaimie had beautiful furniture and a cozy home, but Melissa had been kind of hoping to move into Troy's house soon. Now that dream seemed impossible.

"I mean, like, seriously, he had been kissing me literally two seconds before that, okay, two minutes before that, but still. We were totally making out, and now he's just gone."

"Don't stress, Lizzy. He just needed some time. One of these days, he'll show up at your work or come knocking on the door and everything will be perfect again."

There was a soft knock on the front door, and both girls jumped.

"Do you think that's him?" Melissa asked in panic.

"Who else would be knocking on our door this late at night?" Jaimie asked. "Why don't you go answer it and find out?"

"I can't answer it." Melissa squeaked out a response. "I look terrible. I look like I've been crying all night."

"You *have* been crying all night." Jaimie scrambled to get off the couch and strode across the room to open the door, revealing a very haggard looking Troy Weller. "Good evening, Troy, have you been crying as much as my cousin?"

"Guys don't cry." Troy's gruff voice strained with emotion as he stepped into the living room, slipping off his shoes at the door.

Liar. Melissa didn't stand to greet him, just huddled in the corner of the sofa, not even bothering to wipe the mascara from under her eyes.

"Mind if I sit down?" Troy moved slowly across the room and didn't wait for Melissa to answer his question before lowering into the middle of the sofa, closer to Melissa than to the other side.

She didn't hesitate but climbed right up onto his lap and held him as he wrapped his arms around her and buried his face in her hair. They didn't kiss. They didn't talk. They just held each other.

"Gosh, look at the time," Jaimie said somewhere in Melissa's peripheral thoughts. "I have to work in the morning, so I should probably get to bed."

Neither Troy nor Melissa moved an inch to indicate they'd heard her cousin leave. They just held each other.

Eventually, Troy whispered, "I'm sorry."

"I'm sorry too," Melissa whispered back, not really

sure what she was apologizing for.

"Guess I didn't do as much research as I thought I did," Troy said. "I mean, we've got our Bible Doctrine and Practice explaining our beliefs. You guys need to have a manual or something."

"We do," Melissa said. "It's called the Book of Mormon."

Troy pulled back but kept his arms around her waist. "And you seriously think that's scripture?"

"I know it is." Melissa kept her arms around his neck.

"How do you know?" He still sounded skeptical.

"How do you know the Bible is scripture?"

"Because it just… is," Troy said.

"How do you know?" Melissa asked again.

"I read the Bible every day."

"I read the Book of Mormon every day," she said. "And I cross reference back and forth with the Bible."

"But the Bible contains the teachings of Jesus Christ," Troy said.

"So does the Book of Mormon." Melissa felt as if she were winning this debate, but she had one more point to make. "Have you ever gotten down on your knees and asked God if the Bible is scripture?"

"Asked him? Like ask him ask him?" Troy sounded confused. "Why would I do that? I already know it's scripture."

"How do you *know*?" She knew she was baiting him, but they needed to get past this.

"I don't know how to answer that question," he admitted.

"Can I tell you how I know the Bible is scripture?" Melissa asked, looking him in the eye. He nodded. "Because it feels right. In here." She poked him gently on his chest.

"Yeah, that's a good way to describe it." Troy nodded.

"That's how I feel when I read the Book of Mormon too."

"Can I interrupt?" Jaimie said from the doorway to the hall, holding a little blue book. "When I was serving as a missionary, I gave away dozens of these, and I'd like to gift one to you as well." She stepped tentatively into the room and handed Troy a copy of the Book of Mormon.

"Oh, I couldn't take your book from you." Troy tried to push the book away. "Books are expensive."

"Our church gives them away to anyone who wants one." Jaimie rested the book in Troy's hands.

"If you insist." Troy chuckled and smiled up at Jaimie. "Thank you."

"You're welcome." Jaimie winked at Melissa. "Goodnight."

"I don't know what to say," Troy whispered. "This is a lot to take in."

"I'm sorry." Melissa bit her lower lip.

"You don't have to be sorry." Troy set the book on the little table in front of the couch and wrapped both arms around Melissa, holding her close. "Thank you for being patient with me."

"We'll get through this, Troy," Melissa said. "Just like we'll get through lots of other tough things in this life." Melissa yawned and tucked herself into his arms, resting her head on his shoulder.

"You're exhausted. I should let you get to bed." Troy rubbed her back.

"No, don't leave yet. I just got you back." She snuggled herself even closer.

"Okay." He continued rubbing her back.

"Just hold me a little while longer," Melissa whispered. Her words started to slur.

"Okay," he whispered in a quiet mumble. Within a minute or two, Troy's breathing evened out, slowing to meet her breathing. Before falling asleep, Melissa heard Troy whisper a sleepy, "I love you."

She tried to answer him, but the words never left her thoughts.

Chapter Twenty

Let's Not Talk about Scriptures

Troy woke to the sunlight beaming from the wrong side of the room. He was definitely not in his own bed. Before the thought fully registered, he felt the unmistakable dead weight of Melissa's body resting on top of his.

Oh crud. He didn't want to admit to himself that he had slept with Melissa, but… he had slept with Melissa. In his arms. On top of him. She was still on top of him, thankfully fully dressed. If they hadn't been fully dressed, he might have done the unthinkable. He might have rolled her over and—okay, he needed to go home *right now.*

The noise that escaped his throat was almost a whimper. That, and his uncomfortable shifting underneath her, woke Melissa, and she snuggled closer.

He'd never felt anything so incredible in his life. He'd never felt more tortured in his life. He'd never felt his willpower so tested in his life.

"Melissa," Troy whispered. "I need to go home."

"Okay…" She settled onto his body, and he groaned.

"You're on top of me."

A soft, involuntary smile played across Melissa's full lips, and she hitched her leg up and wrapped herself

109

around him.

"No, no, no." Troy slid out from under her, dropping Melissa onto the sofa, startling her awake.

"Oh my gosh, what are you still doing here?" Melissa's question was laced with panic.

"We fell asleep." Troy scrambled to get away from her before he climbed back onto that couch and kissed her until he couldn't see straight, or worse. He didn't need to have any experience to know there was only one way to make this pain go away, and that was not an acceptable scenario. "I need to leave *right now*."

"When will I see you again?" The vulnerability in her words reminded him that he'd disappeared for several days twice since they started dating. Her concern was justified.

"Soon, I promise," he said, kneeling on the floor beside the couch, his body calming down now that he didn't have the woman he loved draped all over him. "I want to take you over to meet my parents, and I want you to come to church with me, and I want to go to church with you. We need to know more about each other before we jump into marriage. Because to me, marriage is for life. Divorce is not an option."

"Divorce isn't an option for me either." Melissa laid her hand on Troy's cheek. While he turned his head so that he could inhale the essence of her wrist, she continued, "But… uh… in my religion, marriage can be forever."

"That is definitely a difference in interpretation of doctrine," Troy said, kissing the inside of her wrist and seriously reconsidering climbing back onto that couch. "Matthew 22:30 states that in the resurrection, they neither marry, nor are given in marriage."

Melissa sighed and gripped his face tighter. "Yet in Matthew 16:19, it states that whatsoever thou shalt bind on earth shall be bound in heaven. And in Mark 10:9, what therefore God hath joined together, let no man put asunder."

"I would very much like to be joined together with you." Troy's breathing increased as he leaned into her hand and closed his eyes.

"Eternal marriage was taught by a modern-day prophet," Melissa whispered.

"Another point of doctrine on which we disagree." Troy gave up trying to be strong, crushed his lips to Melissa's, climbed back up onto the couch, and pulled her into his arms.

She intertwined her legs with his and gripped his hair, her passion dissolving Troy's willpower.

"Okay, guys, time to come up for air," Jaimie said from the doorway to the living room.

Troy fell off the couch and landed on the floor, glad for the plush carpet, and for the interruption. He startled out of his daze and glanced up sheepishly at Melissa's cousin.

"Melissa and I need to get to our jobs, and I'm sure there's a field somewhere that has a tractor you're supposed to be sitting on."

"A… a field, tractor, right. I'm sure there's

something I'm supposed to be doing right now." Troy sat there on the floor a moment more, trying to regain his bearings.

Melissa hung her face off the side of the couch with a cheesy grin. "Sorry."

Troy leaned close and spoke next to her ear. "Probably shouldn't talk about scriptures together until we're married."

"Probably a good idea." Melissa kissed his cheek, and Troy turned his head, capturing her mouth again.

"Troy, get out of my house!" Jaimie called playfully.

"Yes, ma'am." Troy scrambled away from Melissa, hurried over to the door, and yanked on his shoes without fully tying the laces. He glanced one more time over at Melissa, who was still lying on the couch. "Goodbye, my love."

"Get out!" Jaimie pointed at the door.

Troy was still grinning as he stepped onto the porch, adjusting his clothes and tucking in the parts of his shirt that had gone askew. Trying unsuccessfully to shove thoughts of their kiss out of his mind, Troy looked up to see his brother Craig standing beside his truck, with an angry scowl and arms crossed over his chest. Oops.

Chapter Twenty-one
The Appearance of Evil

"What on earth were you thinking?" Craig's grumble was menacing. His back was resting against the driver's door to Troy's truck and blocking entry.

"We fell asleep, okay?" Troy pulled his keys from his pocket and clicked the key fob to unlock the door. Still, Craig didn't move.

"No, not okay at all," Craig said. "Do you realize how many people know your truck on sight? Everyone. You bought the most identifiable, customized, over-the-top, vanity display of a truck this side of Lansing, and everyone in this town now knows that Troy Weller spent the night with Melissa what's-her-name."

"Melissa's last name is Dalton," Troy said in an unapologetic tone. "And it doesn't matter what anyone else thinks. All that matters is that you're embarrassed of me."

"I'm not embarrassed of you." Craig's tone said otherwise. "I'm disappointed in you. It is my duty as your brother to call you to repentance."

"We didn't have sex, if that's what you're assuming." Troy folded his arms across his chest, mimicking his brother.

"It doesn't matter." Craig pushed himself away from the truck and got in Troy's face. "The appearance of evil is more significant than the deed itself."

"Oh, trust me, it's not," Troy insisted. "Or I wouldn't be in physical pain this morning."

"That is your own fault." Craig narrowed his eyes and took a step back, shaking his head in disgust. "That woman has ruined you. She is a canker to your mind and body. She has turned my innocent brother into a heathen bound for hell."

"I am not a heathen, nor am I bound for hell," Troy said. "Melissa is the best thing that's ever happened to me."

"Your baptism and commitment to the Lord should be the best thing that's ever happened to you."

"My commitment to the Lord is between me and the Lord. He knows my heart, and he knows how strongly I follow his teachings. He loves me, and he forgives me for my mistakes."

"How many times do you think you're going to be forgiven for making the same mistakes?"

"As many times as I'm willing to repent." Troy lifted his chin in defense of God's grace in times of weakness.

"I don't see any admission of guilt or show of repentance in your eyes or in your countenance," Craig said.

"Good thing God only sees what's in my heart and not in my eyes," Troy said. "Besides, all I see in your eyes is judgment. I hope for your soul's sake that's not what's in your heart. And I would suggest you remove the beam from thine own eye before you attempt to remove the mote from mine. If you'll excuse me, I have work to do."

Troy pushed past his brother and opened the door to his truck. While Craig stood in Jaimie and Melissa's driveway with a gaping mouth, Troy gunned his engine and backed out of the driveway. As he headed south out of Lowell, he fought angry tears and lost the battle with one or two of them.

Chapter Twenty-two—The Grace of God

A brotherly kiss upon entering the home of his father was expected and therefore that much more of a slap in the face when not received. Troy knew he was in trouble when he entered the living room and found every seat occupied by other Brethren from the church.

He'd already had a long day in the sun, missed a shower that morning in his haste to get into the field, was hungry and dehydrated. This was the last thing he wanted to endure but found the situation neither unexpected nor unwarranted. What he had done was wrong in God's eyes on so many levels.

Craig pulled up a straight-backed chair and grunted for Troy to sit, which he did.

Their mother, bless her, brought Troy a glass of water and then hurried from the room. He wished he could follow her. He wished he could be anywhere but here.

No one spoke for several long moments as Troy drank heartily of the water his mother had provided, then watched condensation fall in droplets down the sides of the glass, as if the glass had been filled half an hour ago and was waiting as impatiently as the Brethren.

"Father, I'd like to offer my thoughts, if I could." Craig was the first to speak. Great. More condemnation and testimony against him. "As Troy's brother, my duty is to offer admonition and a call to repentance. Troy has shown me through his actions this morning that his heart welcomes the grace and mercy offered by our Lord. I think that should be our first item of discussion this evening."

Huh? Troy gaped at his brother. This was not what he'd expected. Craig lowered his gaze and pursed his lips.

"How are we to preserve the purity of the church if sin is accepted with the least degree of allowance?" The man who spoke up was Becca's father, Timothy. He would be naturally angry at Troy for his rejection of his daughter. "In Galatians chapter five, Paul teaches that the flesh lusts against the spirit, and the spirit lusts against the flesh. These are contrary to one another."

"I agree with the apostle," Troy choked out through his dry mouth. "But if you will hear me out, you'll find that this was not the case in my situation."

"Perhaps we should take a moment to hear Troy's confession before passing judgment," another of the brethren said with pointed direction at the man most likely to desire swift action against Troy. All eyes turned back to Troy, who cleared his throat and set aside the nearly empty glass of water.

"As I'm sure all of you are aware, I've fallen in love with a woman who is not *yet* of our faith." Troy emphasized the word yet in hopes the brethren would acknowledge the importance of sharing the gospel with unbelievers and the acceptance of all children of God. "She loves the Lord and is willing to open her heart to

117

his teachings. She's willing to come to church with me next weekend. I hope that you will all welcome her into the fold. Because in welcoming her, you're welcoming me. In rejecting her… you're rejecting me."

"How so?" Another of the men frowned and folded his arms across his chest.

"I intend to marry Melissa—"

Several of the men gasped. Troy was shocked that any of them hadn't figured that out yet.

"—and in doing so will be excommunicated and removed from your midst."

"That's not what we want for you son," one man mumbled.

"Nor is that what I want," Troy said. "I hope that Melissa will join our fold, and we can become one. She and I have agreed that we need to spend a little more time getting to know each other's faiths before marrying in haste."

"That doesn't explain why you were seen leaving her bedroom this morning," Troy's father said. He hadn't realized his dad was the angriest man in the room. Of all people, Troy expected his own father would desire that his son be offered grace and forgiveness. Apparently, that was not the case.

"Father, I never entered Melissa's bedroom. I was in her cousin's living room and fell asleep on the couch."

"Was Melissa with you on the couch?"

"Yes," Troy choked out.

"Did you sleep together?"

"We slept on the couch together, but we were fully clothed. Nothing happened."

"Were you aroused by her presence?" His father's anger was increasing rather than diminishing.

"Yes." Troy's admission was accompanied by sobs. He rose from his chair and fell to his knees before his father. "I have sinned against heaven and before thee." Troy knew every man in that room would recognize the plea spoken of in Luke by the prodigal son and understand the reference. Troy's heart cried out for mercy and grace.

"Salvation is not obtained through confession." His father's words were wrought with emotion. "But your confession is an outward sign of your broken heart and contrite spirit. Are you willing to turn from your wickedness?"

"I am, Father." Troy sat back on his heels and gazed up at his father with hope of forgiveness.

"The Lord said to the woman taken in adultery to go, and sin no more." He reached for Troy's hand, and Troy grasped on like a lifeline. Then his father lifted his gaze to the brethren in the room. "And the Lord told her accusers that whosoever among them was without sin should be the first to cast a stone."

As Troy clung to his father's hand, he marveled at his father's warning to those who were here to judge that it was time to back down. He felt like a little child laying his head on his father's lap and wrapping his arms around his waist. He whispered, "Thank you,

Father."

His father pushed him away gently. "Uh… Troy?"

"Yeah?" Troy wiped his eyes and found as much grime on his face as tears.

"You need a shower." His father wrinkled his nose but had a gleam in his eyes.

"I do. I know." Troy chuckled and wiped his hands on his grubby jeans.

"Go clean up. Your mother saved you a plate from dinner."

Troy couldn't help connecting the double meaning in his father's command, triple meaning really. His sins would be washed away. He was saved and welcomed among the family. The symbolism was not lost on him, and Troy looked forward to the feeling of being clean again.

Chapter Twenty-three—The Holy Kiss

"Will I be the only woman not wearing a head covering?" Melissa asked, pulling down the vanity mirror in the passenger side of Troy's Ford pickup truck. He had driven north to Lowell to bring her to church rather than making her arrive by herself.

"Nah, there will be a few." Troy glanced over at her, keeping one hand on the steering wheel, and his other elbow leaned on the arm rest between them. "You'll probably be the only woman with her hair down though."

"What?" She had taken twenty minutes curling her long hair into soft ringlets. "Why?"

"A woman's long hair is a glory to her and is given to her for a covering," Troy said. "There are two kinds of head coverings, a natural covering—a woman's hair—and a sign covering, which represents prayer and worship and thus must be something that can be put on and taken off."

"If it's just for prayer and worship, why do women in your church wear the cap all day, every day?"

"Should we not seek to spend all day in Christian service?" Troy asked. "If so, then she should wear the devotional head covering whenever she appears in public as a constant testimony of her submission to God and to her husband."

Melissa wanted to say something about women not being submissive to their husbands, but she held her tongue. No need to cause contention when they were on their way to church.

"I should also tell you about the Holy Kiss," Troy said.

"*The* Holy Kiss?" What did he mean by that?

"The Holy Kiss is used as a Christian Salutation. But don't worry. No one will try to kiss you because you are not of the church."

"Not… uh… holy kiss… uh, okay." As Melissa stammered to grasp the multiple connotations of his statement, Troy turned off the gravel road at a large and modern church building, with a parking lot filling up with pickup trucks and minivans.

"It's a greeting between two brethren in the church, or between two sisters," Troy explained. "From a worldly perspective, the practice may seem strange, but we are not of the world."

"Of course not," Melissa reassured him. "Don't worry about me. I'm not one to judge others."

"The brethren will be welcoming me back into the fold as one who has sinned and repented." Troy pulled his truck to the far corner of the parking lot and parked so that the cab was facing away from the building, providing a moment of privacy to compose themselves before entering the church.

"What did you do?" She laid her hand on his arm.

"I slept with you." His statement was so matter of

fact as if the answer should be obvious.

"But, Troy, we didn't do anything." Melissa scoffed. "All we did was fall asleep."

"But I *wanted* to do things with you. My *body* wanted to do things with you." His intense gaze was sending her a clear message to read between the lines.

"Troy, that's kind of an involuntary thing first thing in the morning, isn't it?" She raised her eyebrows.

"Not like that." Troy shook his head. "That would not have happened if you hadn't been lying on top of me."

"Did you... tell other people about that?"

"They knew. They're all men. They called me out on my sinful behavior."

"Is that considered sinful once we're married?" She hoped not.

"Heck no!" He cleared his throat. "I mean, no, that's not considered sinful once we're married."

She made a show of wiping her brow, and they both chuckled.

"So let me get this straight." Melissa began ticking things off on her fingers. "I'll be the only woman with my hair down and not covered, every guy in the building knows we slept together, and they're all going to kiss you?"

"Very funny." He tugged on one of her curls, then held the strands in his hand and let them slide through his fingers. "But... pretty much, yeah."

"Great, let's do this." Melissa feigned enthusiasm she didn't feel, butterflies fluttering in her stomach.

Troy climbed down from his truck and hurried around to the passenger side to help her down from the cab. Before placing her on the ground, Troy captured Melissa in his arms and pulled her close. "For the record, your hair is beautiful curled like that, I loved sleeping with you, and you are the only person in the world I want to be kissing."

As if to prove his point, Troy captured her lips briefly, and Melissa wished she could remain in that moment, kissing in the church parking lot, relishing in the feeling of being in his arms. Too soon they pulled away, and they took a moment to regain composure.

Before rounding the truck to head toward the front doors of the church building, Troy reached for Melissa's hand. "You ready for this?"

"Nope." She shook her head adamantly but slipped her hand into his and walked with him across the parking lot.

The first people to greet them on the way in the door were Craig and Jessica, who reached out to hug Melissa. Craig, however, placed his hands on Troy's shoulders and wrinkled his nose.

"Really?" Craig shook his head, keeping his hands on his brother's shoulders. He glanced at Melissa and then back to Troy. "That's a lovely shade of lipstick. It looks much nicer on Melissa than it does on you."

"Oh crud." Troy covered his mouth with his hand and glanced at Melissa with wide eyes. "Excuse me while I make a side trip to the men's room."

"Good luck," Melissa called after him as he rushed away. Then she turned to Jessica and giggled. "It's the kind that lasts eight hours."

"Oh, no." Jessica cringed.

"What an idiot," Craig mumbled, then leaned close to his wife. "Glad you don't wear lipstick." He picked up baby Jesse and strode away to go find them a pew.

Melissa and Jessica chuckled again as Becca approached and gave each of them a hug. "What was Troy hurrying off for? Is he sick?"

"He will be when he looks in the mirror," Jessica said.

"He's about to learn the finer aspects of makeup removal." Melissa raised her eyebrows at Becca.

"He didn't…" Becca's jaw dropped.

"He did," Jessica confirmed. "He kissed her."

"In the church parking lot." Melissa nodded.

"What an idiot," Becca said, failing to hide a grin.

"That's what my husband said, too." Jessica wrapped her arm around Melissa. "Come on, let's go sit down. Troy can find us when he gets out of the restroom."

"He's going to be in there awhile." Melissa snickered.

"Serves him right for kissing you before marrying you," Becca said.

"Got that right," Jessica added.

With barely restrained laughter, they headed down the aisle and slid into the pew where Craig had already reserved a spot, leaving space at the end, where Troy slid in at the last minute.

Troy wrapped his arm around the back of the pew and leaned closer to Melissa. "You wanna take off?"

"Nope." She turned and blinked innocent eyes at him. "The lipstick will wear off… in about eight hours."

He shook his head in playful resignation. "Great… just great."

The sermon that morning spoke of purity and cleanliness and the importance of keeping oneself spotless before the world. It was like they'd prepared the sermon just for Troy. Melissa rested her head against his shoulder and sighed, more content than she'd felt in a long time.

Chapter Twenty-four—You Love Me

"I'm disappointed in you, son."

Great, that didn't take long. They'd barely started eating the meal his mother had so graciously prepared for Troy and his new girlfriend, and already his dad was laying into him.

Troy didn't know what to say, so he shoveled in another forkful of baked chicken. He knew his father would want to have his say in the matter before requesting an answer to his accusations. He forked in another bite of food.

His father's glare bounced back and forth between him and Melissa. That woke Troy up a bit. He would not openly defy his father except when the matter affected his wife, well, future wife. Troy swallowed before reacting.

"The fault is mine, Father." Troy wiped his face with his napkin and rested it in his lap. He took Melissa's hand, hoping to convey his solidarity and commitment to her. "I chose to kiss her inappropriately and was punished for my behavior. While attempting to remove the stain, I spent time in sincere repentance for my actions."

"Inappropriately?" Melissa raised her eyebrows at him. "That was a very chaste kiss in a public location, and I don't think God's punishing you because I chose to wear lipstick."

"Young lady, you have no right to presume to know what God does and does not do," Troy's father said. "You are but a harlot tempting our son to stray from the teachings of the church."

"A harlot?" Melissa stood and glared across the table at Troy's father.

"Father, that was uncalled for." Troy stood also, again feeling the need to protect his wife. He tried to wrap his arms around her, but Melissa shook him off.

"Troy, I would like you to take me home please." Melissa didn't even glance up at him as she dropped her napkin over her plate, as if to send a clear message that she didn't plan to eat another bite. "I know where I'm not welcome." She turned on her heel and strode from the room, not even glancing at his mom or thanking her for the nice meal, most of which was still on her plate.

Troy had wanted Melissa to have a chance to get to know his mom, but he knew that his mom wouldn't ever defy her husband and reach out to Melissa. Troy's only choice was to take Melissa home.

"Thanks a lot, Dad." Troy shook his head at his father in disgust, then turned to his mom. "Mother, thank you for the meal. The chicken was delicious." He didn't want to make note of how much chicken was still on his plate or how disappointed he was to leave it uneaten. He left to go find his future wife, hoping the repeated confrontations with his father wouldn't deter her from wanting to marry him.

He found Melissa already sitting in the cab of his

pickup truck, staring straight ahead with a resolute expression. He climbed into the driver's seat and started the engine.

"I suppose that's how you felt when you met my parents, huh?"

"Not even close." Troy turned to face her. "What my dad said was unacceptable and rude. Your parents were polite in comparison."

"I'm sorry," Melissa whispered, her gaze lowered to her lap where her hands were gripping her skirt.

"What do you have to be sorry about?" Troy lifted her chin gently, turning her head toward him.

"We don't belong together, Troy."

"Oh, yes, we do," he said adamantly.

"Every time we turn around, we're creating more problems for ourselves and the people we love. Your family is never going to embrace me, and my family's never going to embrace you, and we'll always argue about which church to take our kids to, and I'll never be good enough for you." With that she lifted her hands from her lap and covered her face, sobbing.

"Listen to me," Troy said, pulling gently on her hands. "You are better than good enough for me. You are perfect for me."

"I'm not perfect, Troy. Nothing about me is perfect." She held firm and continued crying.

"You're perfect *for me*," Troy clarified. "You are the woman God made for me."

"If that were true, why would we have been born into such different lives?" She finally pulled her hands from her face and glared at him. "Look at us. You're a Mennonite. I'm a Mormon. How are we even remotely similar?"

"We both believe in God as the Father, and Jesus Christ, his son, and in God, the Holy Spirit. Right?"

"Yeah, but—"

"But nothing. We both read the Bible, and pray, and we both believe in faith and sin and repentance and baptism and miracles and healings, and we believe that God created the earth and man and woman and plants and animals, and, and, we both love each other."

Melissa met his gaze, and Troy reached up to wipe the mascara from beneath her eyes. "You love me?"

"Of course, I love you," Troy said. "Haven't I made that clear enough yet?"

"I don't know… maybe." The vulnerability in her emerald eyes broke his heart.

"Melissa, I love you. I love you. I love you." He held his hands on either side of her face and pulled her a little closer, hoping she would reciprocate those three magic words.

"Troy, I love you too." She closed the distance between them, and for the second time that day, their lips connected in a forbidden kiss, this time right in his parents' driveway.

Chapter Twenty-five
Marriage Can Be Forever

"Brothers and sisters, the time is now yours to stand and bear your testimonies of the gospel, should you choose," the bishop of the Grand Rapids congregation said into the microphone. "Please keep your comments under five minutes in order to allow time for anyone who feels prompted to share. We'll end the meeting at five minutes to the hour." With that, the bishop returned to his seat and waited with a patient smile.

When Melissa invited Troy to come to church with her, she hadn't realized the Sunday was fast and testimony Sunday. There was no prepared talk or sermon. People were encouraged to share whatever was on their minds or in their hearts. Melissa groaned inwardly. Anything and everything could, and likely would, go wrong with this scenario.

Troy could insist that their religions had enough in common to get them through whatever hard times lay ahead in their lives, but the reality wasn't quite as easy. Melissa ran through a list of things Troy might find confusing or not conforming to his interpretation of Biblical standards.

The Book of Mormon was the most obvious, but also temple marriage, modern prophets and apostles, the restoration of the priesthood, premortal existence, women holding leadership roles in the church, women cutting their hair, women not wearing devotional head coverings, women getting advanced educations. Why did it always have to come down to women's roles? Ugh.

At least everyone was polite and welcoming when Melissa and Troy walked in, hand in hand. They purposely didn't kiss each other in the parking lot and laughed about not making that mistake twice.

Because Melissa hadn't lived in the area for very long, people in the congregation were still trying to get to know her. They wouldn't question her bringing a boyfriend to church.

So far, the meeting had gone okay, other than the conversation following the passing of the sacrament. When the tray of bread was placed in front of him, Troy shook his head.

"I am not allowed to participate in communion observances at your church."

"You can if you want to," Melissa whispered. "We're not like some churches where you have to be baptized into their church before you can take the sacrament."

"I would be excommunicated," Troy stated emphatically.

"Wow, there are a lot of things that will get you excommunicated from your church, aren't there?"

"Not really." He shrugged. "You just happen to be involved in several of them."

"What are they?" Melissa gulped.

"Joining another church, marrying outside the church, and joining the military."

"You're not allowed to join the military?" She tried not to let her eyes stray to the pew several rows over where a young man sat in his dress uniform, having just graduated from basic training in the National Guard and was preparing for deployment to the Southern border to help with the humanitarian crisis. "Why?" She was afraid to ask.

"The Spirit of Christ is in nonresistance, love, gentleness, kindness, patience, goodwill and good works. This is contrary to the spirit of war."

"Okay, well, good to know. I won't encourage you to join the military."

"Kind of a moot point anyway." Troy snickered. "I'll be excommunicated if I marry you."

Melissa didn't like anything about that sentence, particularly the word *if*. Not when. If. Also, she didn't want to be the reason he got kicked out of his church. She turned to face forward, wondering when the next shoe would drop.

The shoe dropped when a nice older woman stepped up to the microphone and shared her testimony about the restored gospel through the prophet Joseph Smith. Melissa had never told Troy the story about Joseph's first vision.

"Young Joseph was confused about which church to join so he knelt in a grove of trees and prayed to ask God which church he should join."

Oh boy, here it comes, Melissa thought. *Troy's not going to like this.*

"Joseph saw a pillar of light over his head, and the light descended to him, and he saw God, the Father, and his Son, Jesus Christ, standing right there in the air."

The old lady's voice was excited and animated.

"They told Joseph not to join any of the churches because they were all wrong."

Not exactly how the story goes, but Melissa had no way of correcting the woman. She glanced sidelong at Troy, gaging his reaction. His brow was creased.

"And that wasn't the only vision Joseph had," the lady continued. "He was visited by resurrected apostles and saw angels, one of whom told him where to find the gold plates containing the writings which were translated and published as the Book of Mormon."

Another thing Troy doesn't want to talk about, Melissa thought.

"I'm thankful to have the restored gospel in my life." The woman glanced over at her husband. "And I'm thankful my husband and I were able to be sealed in the temple to be married for all eternity."

Melissa wished she would be able to say that as well. All her life she'd longed to get married in a temple so that she would be with her husband forever. If she married Troy, she wouldn't have that chance.

Forever marriage wasn't something Troy believed in. He thought marriage ended at death. That was such a sad concept. Melissa felt a tear roll down her cheek and quickly wiped it away.

She thought Troy would put his arm around her and comfort her. She could use reassurance that everything was going to be okay. She could use that confidence Troy had shown last Sunday when he'd stood up to his father in her defense, and when he'd rattled off a list of reasons their religions were similar enough for them to make this work.

Instead of comforting her, Troy did something unexpected. He stood and walked down the aisle, shoved open the doors to the chapel, and left the room.

Chapter Twenty-six—Just Like That?

Troy's mind was racing. His heart was racing. He wanted to race right out to his truck, race from the parking lot, and race home. To his own church. To where he understood the Gospel as taught in the Bible.

He wanted to race home to a place where there were no golden fake scriptures, where the women respected their devotion to God enough to prepare themselves for prayer and worship by properly covering their heads, where men didn't arrive at church wearing war uniforms, where no one spoke of temples and marriages that somehow lasted for eternity.

How was that even possible? There was no logic. And why would Melissa want this temple marriage when she knew she could never have that with him? Did that mean she didn't want to marry him? If she married him, she would be forever resentful that he couldn't marry her in a temple. She would be disappointed. She would hate him.

Troy refused to take that away from her. He refused to be the reason she spent the rest of her life wishing for something she couldn't have.

He hurried down a hallway he thought led to the door where they'd entered the building. Instead, he seemed to be going in a large circle or horseshoe. Wondering if he missed the door, he doubled back and ran right into Melissa. She must have been following him.

"Troy, are you okay?" Melissa's compassionate voice was like a jolt to his already racing heart.

"No, I'm not." He backed away, holding his hands up as if touching her would cause him pain. "This is worse than I thought. You were right. We're too different. We're not meant to be together. There's no way we can make this work."

"Okay," she whispered.

Okay? She wasn't even going to argue? She wasn't going to try to convince him they were meant to be together? She wasn't even going to fight for their relationship? "Just like that?"

"Just like what?" Melissa crossed her arms over her chest, her face a mask of feigned indifference.

"You're not going to even try to convince me to stay with you?" The disappointment was startling to him. Wasn't this what he'd wanted a moment ago?

"Troy, our relationship has been doomed since the day we met," Melissa said with a shrug. "All of our family members have been trying to tell us that, and we refused to listen to them. I think it's time we wake up and smell the manure. This isn't something we can fix with handwashing and a bandage."

"You deserve one of those temple marriage things where you can be with your husband forever." Troy wasn't sure if he was trying to convince her or himself.

"And you deserve to marry someone who won't cause you to get excommunicated." Melissa's point was valid.

"You deserve to read whatever scriptures you want, even if they're written on golden plates." Troy didn't try to hide the derogatory nature of his comment.

"And you deserve to interpret the Bible however you want." Melissa lifted her chin with resolution.

"You deserve to wear your long, beautiful hair down and flowing." He pulled a lock of silken strands through his fingers, letting them slide down and rest across her shoulders.

"And you deserve to marry a woman who's willing to tuck all her hair up into a bun and cover it all day long."

"Our families will be happy we broke up." Troy's words stuck in his throat. Never were words more true.

"Finally, something we agree on." Melissa chuckled with irony.

"Shall I drive you home?" Troy held up the keys to his truck.

"Well, I certainly don't want to walk," Melissa said, turning on her heel and heading back the way they'd come, to a hallway Troy didn't realize led to the outside door.

He followed her and held open the door, relishing the scent of her body lotion. The thought of never experiencing the intoxication of her fragrance nearly crushed his resolve to end this relationship before it got any further out of hand.

The Refusal

Troy kept his hands in the pockets of his dress slacks in an attempt not to hold her hand or wrap his arm around her waist. He did offer his hand to help her up into the cab of his pickup and had a difficult time letting go.

They were quiet on the drive home to Lowell. When he parked in her cousin's driveway, Troy walked around the truck to help her down from the cab. Just as when he'd helped her up, he didn't want to let go. Setting her on the ground, he kept his hands on her hips longer than necessary, begging with his eyes for her to ask him to stay.

She didn't.

Troy backed away and watched Melissa walk up the porch steps to her cousin's house.

She turned one more time to meet his gaze before opening the front door and disappearing within, taking his heart with her.

Chapter Twenty-seven
A Bandage and a Bar of Soap

Work was different from the last time they broke up.

The day they'd driven home from Melissa's parents' house, and Troy had dropped her off at her cousin's, everyone seemed to know they'd broken up. The guys in the community had come out of the woodwork, vying for Melissa's attention.

This time, no one knew they'd broken up.

Not even her cousin.

Melissa went about her daily routine. Got up for work. Spent the day like a zombie. Ran the store. Ordered supplies and inventory. Calculated payroll. Scheduled employee shifts. Volunteered to come early and stayed late. Never made a fuss. Never shed a tear.

It was like Troy Weller never existed. Except, he did exist. And he had changed Melissa. Forever.

And yet, forever is exactly what Troy didn't want. For whatever reason, Troy didn't want to spend forever with her. And for whatever reason, since he didn't want to spend forever with her, he didn't want to spend the rest of his life with her either.

She tried not to let that hurt. She tried not to think about him at all. Or so she told herself.

Not talking about him helped. Since no one knew

they'd broken up, no one gave her those pitying stares.
Since there was no juicy gossip about her and Troy,
everyone went about their daily lives without paying
her any attention.

One week and two days after they broke up, Melissa
had a knock at her office door. Not a face she expected
to see.

"Craig?" Melissa couldn't fathom why Troy's
brother would be showing up at her work in the middle
of a Tuesday afternoon.

"May I have a word with you?" Craig asked. Not
waiting for her answer, he closed her office door and
sat across from her desk. "There's something I need to
tell you."

Their conversation was brief. Ten minutes, tops.
And then he was gone.

And Melissa was left to mop up what was left of her
heart. In order to do that, she needed to make a trip to
the back room and locate a proverbial mop, or in this
case, a green block of industrial strength soap just right
for scrubbing germs out of a hand cut by a broken beer
bottle that destroyed the drive chain on a no-till planter.

As if in a trance, Melissa walked slowly to the utility
sink where she found what she was looking for. She
picked up the strong-smelling bar of green soap and
remembered Troy's comments about how good she
smelled, and how her eyes shone like emeralds. She
never did get that emerald engagement ring.

She held the bar in her hands and turned it over
several times, marveling at the sticky dryness with a

hint of a damp spot on one side.

Melissa turned on the water in the utility sink, holding the soap under the running water, letting the water flow over the bar without fanfare or suds. Rolling the bar over and over, she created a sudsy mound of soap all around her hands, relishing the silky smooth, fluffy bubbles.

After a few moments of scrubbing her own hands, remembering the day she met Troy and how this had felt washing his hands, she set the soap back onto the little rack and rinsed her hands thoroughly. She reached for the paper towel and dried her hands but didn't go so far as to wrap her uninjured hand in a bandage.

She reached into the first aid kit and held an unopened bandage in her hand, welcoming the tears that finally pricked at her eyes. Finally allowing herself to grieve the loss of the man she loved, she sank to the floor in the back room of her store, crouched beside the utility sink and sobbed, rocking back and forth like a confused child.

This is not how she planned to spend her afternoon. This is not how she wanted to live her life. She clutched the unopened bandage in her hand and sobbed.

Chapter Twenty-eight

Gender-confused Chickens

"Judah, quit picking on your sister. Issachar, you'd better get over here and eat before Asher and Naphtali eat all the corn. They're taking the best parts."

Troy held out his hand filled with corn and met the gaze of little Issachar, who was so petite compared to her sisters. He had to conscientiously feed the little girl.

Remembering Melissa's question about his chickens having gender identity issues, Troy wondered how his chickens would feel if they knew he'd named them after boys, well, men. The twelve tribes of Israel.

"You, ladies, don't have a problem with your names, do you? A chicken by any other name is still a chicken, right?" Troy snorted.

This was getting out of hand. He barely ate. He barely slept. He barely worked. The only reason he had to get out of bed each morning was to feed his chickens. They had become his companions and reason for living for days, weeks, no… one week. Or was it two? He'd lost track of time.

"Look at me. I'm sitting in my yard, surrounded by chicken poop and corn and seeds and bits of straw, talking to gender-confused chickens with boys' names. There is something seriously wrong with me. These poor chickens. I need to rename my chickens."

"I like the names of your chickens," a soft voice said from behind him.

He would know that voice anywhere. Dare he turn around and allow the imagined voice to disappear? He chanced the turn of his neck and realized if his ears were imagining Melissa standing behind him, then his eyes were imagining her as well.

"Why is Zebulun way over here where she's not getting any food?" Melissa picked up the little, brown chicken and held her feet in a way that she couldn't escape if she wanted, which she probably didn't. No chicken in her right mind would reject being held by Melissa Dalton.

No man in his right mind would either, which is why Troy knew he'd lost his. Imagining this moment as he'd done over and over, he never dreamed the first sentence out of his mouth would be, "Why did I break up with you?"

"Do you really want me to give you a list?" Melissa stepped up next to him, chicken in her arms, and lowered to sit on the ground, not even looking to see if she'd be sitting in chicken poop. A true farmer at heart.

"No, please don't. Just let me enjoy this fantasy before I wake up and you're not here."

"I don't think that's going to happen," Melissa said with a resigned sigh.

"Why?" Troy's heart was racing.

"Because I refuse to leave this time."

"But what about all the things we disagree on?" Troy

asked, meeting her gaze.

"We'll probably still disagree about them. But we'll wake up in each other's arms and make eggs together."

"What if our parents won't let us get married?" Troy asked.

"Then we'll elope." So matter-of-fact. So logical he wondered why he'd never thought of that.

"What if you never get married in one of your temples?"

"Then we'll be married until death instead of throughout all eternity."

"What if we disagree about whose church to take the kids to each weekend?"

"We'll do one weekend at your church and one weekend at mine."

"What if I'm excommunicated?" He gulped.

"Their loss," Melissa said. "I guess that would narrow our decision about where to take the kids each weekend."

"What if—"

"Troy, stop." She placed her hand over his mouth, effectively shutting him up. "I refuse to let any of that come between us anymore."

"You do?"

"I refuse to let *anything* come between us anymore. It's over. None of it matters. I'm the woman God made for you, and you're the man God made for me, and you're going to marry me—immediately—and you're going to make love to me every night, and wake up with me in your arms every morning, and we're going to raise chickens together, and raise babies together, and serve God together, and live together in a beautiful house overlooking a beautiful farm, where you'll plant the crops and I'll watch my smoking hot husband from our kitchen window, awaiting the hour when you'll come inside to a home-cooked meal and a wife who loves you."

"When you put it that way, we should have gotten married a long time ago." Troy grinned.

"We weren't ready," Melissa said.

"What changed your mind?" Troy asked.

"Your brother stopped by the store and told me you'd gone a little… off your rocker. He said you weren't handling our breakup well and that I needed to get my act together and get over here and whip some sense into you."

"Why would he do that?" No wonder he was having this daydream fantasy. He was insane. His brother had already informed Melissa that he was insane so it must be true.

"He's concerned about you," she said with compassion. "He told me that if I didn't take the initiative, I'd be throwing away both of our chances for happiness."

"And it doesn't bother you that I'm insane and talking to chickens?"

"Didn't you hear me?" Melissa asked. "I refuse to let that stop us."

Troy lifted Zebulun out of Melissa's hands, gave the chicken a little toss, and off she flew to land among her sisters, fighting her way into the pecking order.

Not taking into consideration that he may or may not be dreaming, or the fact that they were sitting in a yard surrounded by chicken poop and crushed corn and clucking chickens happily enjoying their dinner, Troy turned to his future bride and pulled her into his arms, gripping his hands into her hair and connecting his lips to hers.

If this was a dream, he never wanted to wake up.

Epilogue—Final Refusal

Their newly built pole barn near their newly built house had yet to be defiled by any tractors, cars, tools, animals, or people. The poured concrete floor had yet to receive even a single stain from oil. The walls didn't have a single cobweb. The darn thing even smelled new.

Until the caterers arrived with the food. The main dish, pot roast, of course.

The decorations were simple. The folding chairs were lined up in rows at the beginning of the wedding, and pushed to the side for the reception.

Melissa's dress was modest enough to be worn to the temple or to a Mennonite church, even though they were married in a pole barn filled with a diverse collection of guests who mostly disagreed with their decision to be married.

Troy and Melissa didn't care. They refused to let their friends and family members sway their decision.

Troy's minister declined to marry them, and there was still the looming threat of excommunication. Troy refused to let that sway his decision.

Melissa's bishop was willing to officiate even though they realized the sealing power of the temple ceremony would not be included and the marriage would last for the rest of their lives rather than the rest of eternity. Melissa refused to let that sway her decision.

They refused to let anything, or anyone come between them.

The wedding was held on a Friday evening, a few days after they'd been given final approval and the keys to their new home. Forget a hotel. They had the most beautiful view of the landscape from the kitchen window, and beautiful curtains and shades in the bedroom window, which they didn't intend to open for a long, long time.

After they'd eaten the obligatory number of bites of food and cake, taken the obligatory number of photographs, and hugged the obligatory number of guests, they kicked their family and friends off their property and Troy carried Melissa over the threshold of the door to their new home.

The carpet had never been walked on, the dishwasher had never been run, the laundry machine had never been used, and the bed had never been slept on... yet.

Troy set Melissa on the floor near the entrance to their bedroom and leaned against the wall near the door. "Can I tell you a secret?"

"I hope you're comfortable telling me anything," Melissa whispered, suddenly more nervous than she had been at the prospect of finally being alone with her groom.

"I didn't want to get married."

"What?" The butterflies in her center turned into thumping in her ears.

"Until I met you." A sly smile grew on Troy's face.

"Really?" Melissa blew out a long, shaky breath. "But I'm not exactly the kind of wife you dreamed of in your youth."

"Exactly."

"Huh?"

"I have devoted my life to serving God, and to serving the land, and my community, and my church. But getting married wasn't a priority to me. I didn't spend my youth dreaming of the perfect wife."

"What changed your mind?"

"You." Troy lowered his head so that he was looking her in the eye. "You changed my mind, and my heart. You punched a hole into my world and challenged everything I thought I knew about life."

"You confirmed everything I thought I knew about life," Melissa said, eliciting a confused crease on Troy's brow. "I'm headstrong and determined to live on my own terms and not be seen as just a beautiful woman."

"Hard to hide the beauty of an angel in white," Troy said, his eyes playfully traveling the length of her wedding gown.

She ignored his teasing. "You've shown me that it's okay to be a beautiful woman."

"I have?" Troy pulled her into his arms. "How have I shown you that it's okay to be a beautiful woman?"

"You have shown me that I'm a chosen vessel of God, prepared to bring your babies into the world and raise them and love them and protect them… while you protect me."

The teasing was gone from his countenance, and his eyes searched hers. His whisper was sincere, "I promise to protect you… and our babies."

"I know we won't always agree on everything," Melissa said. "And I know there will be struggles and challenges as we grow together in our marriage. But I truly believe that God directs your path and that you live your life according to his plan for you."

"I try," Troy whispered, his voice wavering but his gaze never leaving hers.

"Troy, I honor you as head of our household and as the spiritual leader in our home." Melissa felt a peace come over her heart, and a single tear fell from each of her eyes. She took a deep breath and continued. "I will follow wherever you lead."

"I will lead you in righteousness." The intensity of Troy's statement hung in the air, and Melissa felt warmth from her heart, emanating to the very tips of her toes. Her fingers trembled as she pulled his face down to hers.

A passionate kiss sealed their commitment to one another. The rest of the night was too sacred for words, but the love they shared would forever remain in their hearts.

Love Letter
from Author Julie L. Spencer

Oh, my friends, I love these characters. They are so special to me. I hope you love them too.

Why do I do this to myself? Why do I write such controversial books?

You may know by now that I am a member of The Church of Jesus Christ of Latter-day Saints (commonly referred to as Mormons for short, however much of a misnomer that is since we worship Jesus Christ not the prophet Mormon).

So why am I writing a book with a main character who is a Mennonite?

Because of my friend Troy (last name withheld for confidentiality). He was at my office one day a few years ago and I made a flippant comment about a man in my office who wasn't treating me very well and looked down upon me for being a headstrong woman.

I am a headstrong woman. Probably to a fault.

I'm a headstrong businesswoman who's taking on the world and standing up for the causes I believe in. I'm fighting for justice on behalf of the people and natural resources of our community. I'm a scientist. I'm a lobbyist. I'm a fighter.

But I also honor my husband as the head of my household just like Troy's wife presumably honors him as the head of her household.

The man I don't honor is the jerk who was treating me poorly at my office. He's gone now. He left years ago. I'm pretty sure he doesn't even live in the State of Michigan anymore. Good riddance. No man should ever treat a woman (or anyone) with disrespect. No one, male or female, should treat anyone else, male or female, with disrespect. I tend to believe that my friend Troy would agree with me on that.

But when I admitted that I'm a headstrong woman, Troy asked me, (I'll never forget his words so I'm putting them in quotation marks!) he asked me, "How does that work out at home?"

That stopped me in my tracks, and I was speechless.

Did I not just state a moment ago that I honor my husband as the head of my household? Do most women honor their husbands as the head of their household? If you're ready to say something snippy to me about how men and women are created equal, let me ask the question of you, Is that really true?

Men and women are extremely different. I don't need to launch into an anatomy and physiology lesson here for you to visualize what I'm talking about.

Is one better or worse? No, we're different.

Women are God's chosen vessels on this earth. We are the only gender able to have children. We are the only gender able to willingly agree to have a spirit body enter a tiny little physical body and carry that little physical body inside our larger physical body, endure an incredible amount of pain in order to push that little body into the big, scary world and then we hold that little body in our arms, crying with happiness that he or she was entrusted to us to nurse and love and teach and help become a larger physical body who will someday create more little physical bodies and bring them into the world to house God's spirit children.

And who is going to protect us (as mothers) as we protect these little physical bodies? It's not a trick question. You can say it out loud. Who has God asked to stand as protectors of the mothers chosen to create these little physical bodies? Our husbands.

If not our husbands, then who? Should we hire a bodyguard? I love my husband. He's way more than a bodyguard. He treasures me, not just as the woman who willingly accepted the little physical bodies who house the spirits we call our children. He LOVES me. I would not want any other person on this planet to stand as my protector. He provides for me. He goes to his job every day and brings home money that can be used to support me and our children. He would rather work two jobs than to ask me to hire someone else to nurse our children so that I can help bring in money to support our household.

So when Troy asked me, "How does that work out at home?" I realized, I'm not like this at home. I'm not a headstrong businesswoman who's taking on the world and standing up for the causes I believe in. I'm not fighting for justice on behalf of the people and natural resources of our community. I'm not a scientist. I'm not a lobbyist. I'm not a fighter.

Because I don't have to be.

The Refusal

I can come home and take off the business suit, and let someone else protect me for a change. I can snuggle into my husband's arms and let him protect me. He can make the decisions for just a little while. He can lead me and help me and care for me. And he's good at that. Because that's the way God made him.

Troy didn't tell me that's how it should be. He merely reminded me that my husband is there for me.

So, thank you, Troy for asking that poignant question that I haven't forgotten to this day. Is it any wonder that I had to name my character after you? You're old like me. I don't know what you were like as a young man. My character may not be anything like you. My character is not a real person. But he was inspired by you.

I hope that my story, called *The Refusal*, does justice to the teachings of both our religions and the gospel principles we hold to be true. You may not agree with how I chose to end the book, but that's okay. The book is fiction. The characters are not real. But maybe something in this story will touch your heart in the same way that your poignant question touched mine.

This was a tough book to write. I needed to make sure that I conveyed the message that both families wish their children will marry within the faith without portraying either religion as being less than or more than the other.

The main female character, Melissa, will not be excommunicated if she marries outside her church, but the main male character, Troy, will (unfortunately). I did not show that within the pages of this book, but it was made clear, and it is a source of heartbreak. Just like Troy doesn't want to take Melissa away from the fellowship of her church, Melissa had similar feelings. This is one of the many challenges that almost broke them up.

One challenge I faced in writing this book was to make sure I stayed true to the strong gospel principles of both faiths without allowing readers to see either religion as being backward or not keeping up with the times.

God's laws do not change based on what is politically correct, but political correctness can change readers' opinions about me as an author and both churches' gospel principles. I have tried my best to package all of this into something enjoyable to the correct readers. I can't please everyone, but I will try to please my readers. I'd love your thoughts and opinions.

Did you love *The Refusal*? The greatest gift you could ever give me is to leave a review on Amazon and/or Goodreads. Even if you didn't purchase this book for yourself, you can still leave a review. Even just a couple of sentences telling the world what you liked or didn't like can help others decide if they want to read the book. While you're considering whether to leave a review, please enjoy the first chapter of *The Cove*.

God bless you, my friends. Stay safe! *-Julie L. Spencer*

Featured Book: The Cove

The Cove is the book that started my author career!

Get to know Gail Pederson, the selfish, spoiled brat who destroyed the lives of the three men who loved her, and (almost) lived to tell about it! Happy reading!

(Might want to grab a box of tissue.)

Chapter One

"Why did you do that?" Gail stood in his lit doorway, dripping wet in her designer swimsuit. Todd kept the screen door closed between them, anger in his eyes and a scowl on his face. Gail pushed the door open and stomped into his house, leaving water all across his linoleum floor. He closed his eyes, took a deep breath, then grabbed the kitchen towel from the handle on the stove. As he stooped down to wipe up the mess, she grabbed her long hair in her hands and wrung the water from it so that it left an even bigger pool of water beside her. He paused, clenched his hand around the towel and wiped up that mess as well. When Todd stood up, he tossed the towel at Gail's chest.

"Dry yourself off." Todd snapped at her. "You're making a mess in my kitchen." He walked back over to the counter where he had been making himself a sandwich. *How can he possibly be hungry after all that food at the country club?*

"Why did you have to show up there anyway?" Gail demanded.

"I was invited!" Todd turned back to her with fierceness in his eyes. "By your *fiancé!*" He spat the words at her and she flinched back from his accusing eyes. He stepped away from the counter and crossed the room to her. She was glad he'd put down the knife he'd used to cut the salami for his sandwich. Not that she thought he would ever really get so mad he might hurt her, it just would have felt a little more threatening.

"Stephan invited…you? Why?" He ignored her question.

"Do you have *any* idea how much Patrick loves you? How much it's going to hurt him when he finds out that you're *engaged* to someone else?"

She backed away from him, turned and walked into the dining room, looking around for someplace she could sit that wouldn't leave a wet stain. Todd followed her and seemed to anticipate what she needed. He moved a stack of books off a dining room chair that was vinyl or plastic or some other surface she didn't really care to know about. Nothing in her sheltered little world would contain anything so *cheap*, but at that moment she didn't really care. She was just glad to get off her feet.

Gail suddenly realized how tired she was, not just from swimming but from the whole day. Without really consciously thinking about it, she realized she was tired from the past few weeks, months, maybe years. She was just tired. She rested her arms on the table and leaned her head forward. He left the room and came back with a big, fluffy towel and draped it around her shoulders.

"Thanks." She looked up at him. The scornful expression still had not left his face. That hard look in his eyes told her he was far more angry with her than she was with him.

Patrick was Todd's best friend, had been since a Boy Scout trip in their early teens. They had hung out at every Stake activity, every Youth Conference, every camping trip. They were best buddies, and Gail had just hurt his best buddy more than she'd ever hurt anyone before. The tricky part was...Patrick didn't even *know* about it yet. He was still serving as a missionary in the Philippines.

It was the classic case of girl waiting for her missionary, girl meeting another guy who already returned from his mission, girl being wooed into a relationship quicker than she knew what hit her, and girl being proposed to at a dance.

"I didn't mean to say yes..."

"What?"

Gail flinched away from Todd's demanding glare.

"Well, what would you do if someone proposed to you in front of two hundred people?" she asked in exasperation. "Including your mom and dad!" She buried her face in her arms again and started crying. He stood there for a moment, then she heard him stomp from the room. When he came back he set something on the table beside her.

"Here!" He snapped when she didn't look up. She raised her head and gratefully accepted a box of tissues. "How did you get here, anyway?"

"I swam." Gail sniffed and wiped her nose.

"All the way across the cove?"

"It's not that far." She grabbed a couple more tissues and dried the remaining tears. "I train everyday and swim at least that and more."

"Yeah, but that's in a pool. Isn't it a little different?"

"Not really." She sat up a little straighter and began towel-drying her hair. She wanted to be angry still, but decided she really didn't have that much to be angry about. She was more embarrassed than anything else. There she had been, dancing with Stephan at the country club when suddenly he had hopped up on the band stand, grabbed the microphone from the lead singer, stopped the band and called out to her across the room.

Gail was petrified when she realized what he was about to do. She was rooted to her spot on the dance floor but looked over at where her mom and dad were sitting. They were beaming! They loved Stephan. He was everything they would ever want for their little girl. He was in his last year of college, worked at her father's firm, had been home from his mission for three years, and was ready to settle down. He came from a good family, which translated in her parents' minds as a *rich* family, was handsome and confident and someone they could trust to take care of their daughter.

Gail had reached her hand up to her neck as if to grasp the set of pearls that rested there. And Stephan had asked her to marry him. She felt tears fall from her eyes as a completely different future flashed in front of her. A future filled with parties just like this one, filled with an extravagant home and children who were just as beautiful as Stephan. *A future without Patrick.* She was so uncertain at that moment, with everyone staring at her waiting for her reply.

She had smiled back at Stephan and nodded her head, agreeing to marry him. He ran across the room and swooped her up in his arms. He swung her around and the audience cheered. Gail couldn't help smiling and laughing until he put her down and she caught the eye of someone she never would have expected to see at the country club. There, on the other side of the room, standing with a plate of appetizers in one hand and a glass of punch in the other, was Todd.

Gail hadn't seen Todd since Patrick left for his mission. Todd was best friends with Patrick. Her missionary. The boy she had planned to wait for. The boy she had known and loved since their days in Primary. The boy who was counting on her to be there when he got home, just four short months from now. Was four months so long to wait? Could she not endure that long? She realized it wasn't even that she couldn't wait. She never had intended for any of this to happen.

Gail had met Stephan in the gym at the college where they were both students. He knew that she swam every morning, and he knew that he wanted to meet her. Conveniently, he decided that he needed to swim every morning at that same time.

Gradually, they became friends and realized their parents were both members of the same country club, and Stephan worked in her father's law firm.

Gail started spending time with Stephan and they went to dances together and to parties at the club. Every church activity she attended, he was there. Every Institute class, every sacrament meeting. Suddenly he was everywhere she was, and she didn't seem to mind. Stephan was a great guy. He encouraged her with her swimming, and her studies, and was just an all-around decent man. But...he wasn't Patrick.

Gail had continued to write to Patrick faithfully all along. She had always been careful not to get too romantic in her letters. She'd been warned not to do that to missionaries. They needed to concentrate on their work. She really hadn't even made any firm commitments to Patrick before he left. There was just an unspoken connection. They had held hands at recess in elementary school. They had gone to prom together. They had been each others' first kiss. They had loved one another longer than either of them could remember. They were comfortable together.

Up until that night, Gail's letters to Patrick had gone out once a week for the past year and a half. What was going to happen now? Would she write him a "Dear John" letter like she'd heard so many other girls had done? She needed some good advice. She felt confusion mix with her exhaustion and she laid her head back on her arms and closed her eyes.

"How do you know Stephan, anyway?" Gail suddenly looked up at Todd. It occurred to her she knew very little about what Todd had been doing since the last time she'd talked to him over a year and a half ago at Patrick's farewell.

"I have a couple of classes with Stephan at the college." He sat down across from her.

"Are you in business school then?" she asked. She doubted it. He didn't look like the corporate type. He was tall and solid. He was tanned like he spent a lot of time outdoors.

"Economics, with a minor in Business Administration. I'm in my senior year, but probably won't graduate till December. I'm a little behind still."

"Seriously?" she asked. "You're awfully young, aren't you? How did you get through college so fast?"

"I'm older than you think I am." Todd leaned his arm against the table. "I'm three years older than Patrick. I just served in Venture Scouts well into my college years because I lived at home while I was going to school. So, I stayed really close to the guys. Plus I got two years in at the college before I went on my mission."

"Hmmm, you'd think I would have known that. I've known you for years."

"You're kind of caught up in your own little world."

"What are you saying? That I'm a snob and don't pay attention to the people around me?" She stuck her chin in the air, slightly offended yet realizing there may be a ring of truth to it.

"No, I'm just saying you're really busy with all of your…activities."

"You don't approve of how much time I spend at the pool, do you?"

"I think it's honorable that you want to achieve so much. The Olympics were a big deal. You impressed the heck out of all of us." He paused. "You know I attended almost every meet you had locally, with Patrick?"

"I didn't know that, sorry."

"Like I said, you're busy."

"Do you work? Or are you finishing school first?" she asked.

"I'm a builder. I'd like to own my own company someday. That's why I'm going to business school."

That would explain the tan and the physique. It occurred to Gail she was sort of staring at him with a little wonder on her face. She felt her cheeks heat up and looked away.

"What are you going to do now?" Todd asked.

"I don't know." Gail let out a tired sigh, then stood up to leave. "I'll have to think about that. Don't say anything to Patrick about this yet, okay? Or Stephan."

"All right," he said, pushing back from the table. "I should probably drive you home though. You look like you're about ready to fall over from exhaustion." He led her out of his tiny cottage and helped her climb up into his Ford F-250.

It seemed a little strange to Gail that Todd had such meager accommodations, yet a brand new, fancy truck with all the features and gadgets a guy could ever want.

As he walked around the car, she couldn't help draw in a deep breath and lean her head back against the leather seat. His truck smelled amazing. The mixture of new-car smell and whatever cologne he wore was intoxicating. When Todd got into the truck, he didn't seem to notice she was impressed with it. It seemed like it was just a truck to him. *Maybe he needs a big truck for his work as a builder. It's probably a guy thing.*

It took longer than she would have thought to follow the coastline back to her house, and it occurred to her that the cove probably was larger than she realized. Still, the swim had felt good. It hadn't been too far. She was an experienced swimmer, an Olympic gold medalist with a world record in the 400 meter freestyle.

She had been approached by several sponsors after her most recent win, but had settled on Speedo and All Sport. She had always worn Speedo's swimwear and knew the quality and styles. She felt comfortable endorsing them, and they had offered her a lot of money to pose for photo shoots. Also, she liked one of All Sport's sports drinks and she just wanted to support what she used.

Gail had renounced her collegiate eligibility in order to cash in on endorsement offers, but felt it was cool that so many sponsors had approached her. She drifted off in her own thoughts as they drove, and she realized she kind of thought of herself as a little invincible when it came to swimming. Pulling into her driveway brought her out of her daze.

"Don't take me all the way to the house," she asked him.

"Why? Are you embarrassed to be seen with me?"

"No." She laughed. "I just left my clothes down by the water. I took off that stifling dress before launching myself into the lake to come over and yell at you." Something about telling him that made her blush again, and she wondered why she should feel bashful around him. He was just a friend. A friend of her boyfriend…well former boyfriend. And a friend of her…fiancé. That was going to take some getting used to.

"Um, just curious…" He pulled around the bend of her driveway, completing a perfect three-point turn rather than start up the hill towards the house. "Were you wearing your swimsuit under your dress? I probably shouldn't have asked you that. I'm sorry. I'm just dead curious." He stammered on until Gail was doubled over with laughter.

"Of course I had my swimsuit on. I always have a swimsuit on. I pretty much live in one. You don't have to be embarrassed." She jumped down out of his truck and ran lightly across the grass to where her heap of clothes lay by the seawall. She picked up her heels and dress from the dew covered grass and turned back to wave goodbye to Todd. He was already backing up to finish his turn back down the driveway and out of her world.

Gail's attention was drawn back to the dark water of the cove, then up the hill to her home and the country club next door. Gail had grown up at that club, had learned to swim, had first been approached by a coach who wanted to train with her. The party there was still in full swing. Party was a relative term anyway. What her parents and their friends did was mainly dancing and eating. That had been the plan for her evening as well.

It was interesting how her life had taken a drastic turn. What had started as a casual relationship with a nice man had suddenly become an engagement. Her planned future with Patrick had vanished into a distant dream. A new future loomed in front of her and she had gone from being Patrick's girlfriend to being Stephan's fiancé.

She smiled and sighed in contentment as she thought of Stephan. He was an amazing man and someone she would be proud to call her own. She thought of the smile on his face as she agreed to become his wife, but her thoughts quickly turned to Todd's face as he realized what had happened. The anger she remembered changed in her mind to a calm expression of understanding. She wondered why her thoughts would take such a sudden turn. Gail's eyes were once again drawn to the cove and across the lake to the small cottage where Todd's truck was just pulling into his driveway.

Acknowledgments

Lisa Rector, I could never thank you enough for your editing skills. You truly save me time and again from publishing stories with huge, gaping holes, and commas in all the wrong places.

Thanks, Lisa Rector for another fabulous cover design. You outdo yourself over and over.

Audrianna Anderson, thank you for being my right-hand woman, administrative assistant, personal assistant, virtual assistant, social media coordinator, sounding board, cheerleader, sometimes-counselor, and true friend.

Thank you, Lara Wynter, for reading my books from the other side of the world and telling me how this story would be different if told from Australia. Also, for helping me fix some things to be more understandable for my international readers. Let's rock!

To my Chapter-A-Day super fans, particularly Joel Rees, Laura Palmer, Paula Hurdle, Bonnie Congrove-Fritz, Teya Peck, Julie Berryman, Lori Smith, Sally Pomerantz, and Crissy Holland. You give me a reason to write every day and fix my mistakes on the fly.

Most especially, thank you to God and to my husband, children, and family. You are my inspiration.

-Julie L. Spencer

About the Author

Julie L. Spencer writes gritty clean fiction with snarky, flawed characters, and romantic twists and turns. She has over 30 publications, and the books just keep writing themselves. A scientist by day and moonlighting as an author, Julie is an indoor girl with very little desire to step away from her computer and loves her characters almost as much as she loves her kitten.

Sign up for Julie's email newsletter at
www.subscribepage.com/author-julie-spencer

Julie loves to hear from her readers and can be reached at
julie@spencerpublishingLLC.com

Check out Julie's website at:
www.authorjuliespencer.com

Other books by Julie L. Spencer:

All's Fair in Love and Sports Series

Running to You

Meet Me at Half Court

Pass Me the Ball

Basketballs and Mistletoe

Strike Three, You're Mine

Cheer for Me

Catching Waves with You

Matching You with Love

(with co-author Audi Lynn Anderson)

Royal Family Saga Series

Billionaire Crown Prince

Billionaire Hero

Billionaire Professors (The Geek Twins)

Billionaire's Brother

Billionaire's Sons

Julie L. Spencer

Love Letters Series

Who Wants to Marry a Mormon Girl?
Who Wants to Marry a Billionaire Gamer?

Rock Star Redemption Series

Almost a Rock Star
Billionaire Rock Star
International Rock Star
Fallen Rock Star
Forever a Rock Star
Opening Act: Infusion Deep Meets Buxton Peak
(with co-author, Lara Wynter, Free on Amazon)

Christian Romance

The Cove
The Man in the Yellow Jaguar
The Farmer's Daughter
The Refusal

Social Issues

Combustion

Hidden Swan

Listen to audiobooks by Julie L. Spencer:

All's Fair in Love and Sports Series

Running to You on Audible

Meet Me at Half Court on Audible

Pass Me the Ball on Audible

Basketballs and Mistletoe on Audible

Strike Three, You're Mine on Audible

Love Letters Series

Who Wants to Marry a Mormon Girl? on Audible

Who Wants to Marry a Billionaire Gamer? on Audible

Rock Star Redemption Series

Almost a Rock Star on Audible

Billionaire Rock Star on Audible

International Rock Star on Audible

Fallen Rock Star on Audible

The Refusal

Forever a Rock Star on Audible

Christian Women's Fiction

The Cove on Audible
The Man in the Yellow Jaguar on Audible

www.ingramcontent.com/pod-product-compliance
Lightning Source LLC
Chambersburg PA
CBHW051518170626

46811CB00002B/888